Abandoned —on the— Wild Frontier

Trailblazer Books

Gladys Aylward • *Flight of the Fugitives*
Mary McLeod Bethune • *Defeat of the Ghost Riders*
William & Catherine Booth • *Kidnapped by River Rats*
Governor William Bradford • *The Mayflower Secret*
John Bunyan • *Traitor in the Tower*
Amy Carmichael • *The Hidden Jewel*
Peter Cartwright • *Abandoned on the Wild Frontier*
Elizabeth Fry • *The Thieves of Tyburn Square*
Jonathan & Rosalind Goforth • *Mask of the Wolf Boy*
Sheldon Jackson • *The Gold Miners' Rescue*
Adoniram & Ann Judson • *Imprisoned in the Golden City*
Festo Kivengere • *Assassins in the Cathedral*
David Livingstone • *Escape from the Slave Traders*
Martin Luther • *Spy for the Night Riders*
Dwight L. Moody • *Danger on the Flying Trapeze*
Samuel Morris • *Quest for the Lost Prince*
George Müller • *The Bandit of Ashley Downs*
John Newton • *The Runaway's Revenge*
Florence Nightingale • *The Drummer Boy's Battle*
Nate Saint • *The Fate of the Yellow Woodbee*
Menno Simons • *The Betrayer's Fortune*
Mary Slessor • *Trial by Poison*
Hudson Taylor • *Shanghaied to China*
Harriet Tubman • *Listen for the Whippoorwill*
William Tyndale • *The Queen's Smuggler*
John Wesley • *The Chimney Sweep's Ransom*
Marcus & Narcissa Whitman • *Attack in the Rye Grass*
David Zeisberger • *The Warrior's Challenge*

Also by Dave and Neta Jackson

Hero Tales: A Family Treasury of True Stories From the Lives of Christian Heroes (Volumes I, II, & III)

99A

Abandoned —on the— Wild Frontier

Dave & Neta Jackson

Story illustrations by
Julian Jackson

BETHANY HOUSE PUBLISHERS
MINNEAPOLIS, MINNESOTA 55438

Abandoned on the Wild Frontier

Story illustrations by Julian Jackson.
Cover design and illustration by Catherine Reishus McLaughlin.

Published by Bethany House Publishers
A Ministry of Bethany Fellowship International
11400 Hampshire Avenue South
Minneapolis, Minnesota 55438
www.bethanyhouse.com

Printed in the United States of America by
Bethany Press International, Minneapolis, Minnesota 55438

Library of Congress Cataloging-in-Publication Data

Jackson, Dave
Abandoned on the wild frontier / Dave and Neta Jackson ; text illustrations by Julian Jackson.
p. cm. — (Trailblazer books ; 16)
Summary: His friendship with Peter Cartwright, a Methodist circuit-rider evangelist, enables thirteen-year-old Gil to pursue his dream of locating his mother who was kidnapped by the Sauk Indians during the War of 1812.

1. Cartwright, Peter, 1782–1872—Juvenile fiction.
[1. Cartwright, Peter, 1782–1872—Fiction. 2. Clergy—Fiction. 3. Sauk Indians—Fiction. 4. Indians of North America—Middle West—Fiction]
I. Jackson, Neta. II. Jackson, Julian, ill. III. Title. IV. Series.
PZ7.J132418Ab 1995
[Fic]—dc20 95–10049
ISBN 1–55661–468–3

CIP
AC

There is no record of Black Hawk and his braves taking prisoners back to Illinois from the War of 1812, though taking captives was quite common among most tribes.

Gilbert Hamilton, his mother, and the whole Hamilton family are fictional. However, Gilbert coincides with a real person in his role as the wagon driver (unnamed in all the records) whom Cartwright hired to help move his family to Illinois. Robbie and George Hamilton also coincide with real people in the "cornstalk duel."

While some of the incidents involving Cartwright's travels and ministry occurred on dates other than those ascribed in this narrative, all are authentic. Also, the events from the War of 1812, Cartwright's interactions with Andrew Jackson and Abraham Lincoln, and his establishment of the Potawatomi Mission are true.

DAVE AND NETA JACKSON are a husband/wife writing team who have authored or coauthored many books on marriage and family, the church, and relationships, including the books accompanying the Secret Adventures video series, the Pet Parables series, and the Caring Parent series.

They have three children: Julian, the illustrator for the Trailblazer series, Rachel, a college student, and Samantha, their Cambodian foster daughter. They make their home in Evanston, Illinois, where they are active members of Reba Place Church.

CONTENTS

The Wild Frontier
About 1824

Chapter 1

Refuge in a Rain Barrel

As soon as she heard the first pop, pop, pop of the distant muskets, the young mother extinguished the morning fire and closed and barred the cabin's shutters. Maybe, with the cabin closed up, the attackers would think she had fled into the nearby village for safety. She scooped her four-year-old son out of his bed and sat with him in her rocker. By the light of a single lamp she softly sang,

I see the moon,
and the moon sees me.
God bless the moon,
and God bless me.

There's grace in the cabin
And grace in the hall,
And the grace of God is over us all.

"Mommy," interrupted little Gilbert sleepily, "where's Papa?"

"He's with the other men of the village and all those Kentucky soldiers who came to help us. They're trying to fight off the British and Indians."

"Will he come home soon?"

"I hope so."

The sound of cannons boomed above the steady crackle of rifle fire as the fighting got closer. Audry Hamilton could now hear the yells and screams of men in battle. She rocked faster and sang her song again, her voice sounding thin and strained. Suddenly she stopped. "Wait here," she said, putting Gilbert in the chair and going to the door. She removed the bar and peeked out, then slammed it.

"Come here, son." Moving swiftly, she pulled the last blanket out of an old trunk and wrapped it around the boy who had obediently followed her. "I'm going to hide you where no one can find you."

The boy rubbed his eyes with the back of his hands. "But I don't wanna be hidded away," he whined, sticking out his lower lip. "If you hide me, I'll be lost like my spinning button. I can't find it!"

"Hush, now . . . don't worry. I won't lose you," soothed his mother. "I just want to keep you safe."

With that she picked up the child, wrapped tight like a papoose, and headed for the door. On the way she grabbed a couple of hair-on deerskins off the bed, opened the door a crack, then hurried outside and around to the back of the cabin. Behind the cabin, not more than a hundred yards away, was the village of Frenchtown surrounded by its flimsy stockade.

She thought of making a run for it, but the closest gate was around to the north, and more fighting could be heard in that direction.

"Where are you going to hide me?" came the child's muffled voice from inside the bundle.

"Shh. I . . . I . . ." She looked around. "I'm gonna put you in the rain barrel," she finally gasped. "But you mustn't make a sound. No one will find you."

"But what if it rains? I don't wanna get wet. I might drown!" The boy began wiggling.

"Stay still," Audry whispered loudly. "There's no rain in the middle of January in Michigan." She put the bundle down on the snow and pulled the lid off the barrel.

Into the bottom she threw one of the deerskins. Then she lifted the boy in and wedged the other deerskin around him.

By this time the fighting was getting noticeably closer. *Probably just across the meadow,* thought the anxious woman.

"I can't move," Gilbert complained.

"You don't need to move," snapped his mother. "Just stay put and be quiet. I'm going to put the lid back on. Plenty of air will come through the hole for you to breath. Now hush!"

With that she plunked the lid back on the barrel

and hurried back around to the cabin door.

The morning mists were rising over the snow-covered meadow in front of the cabin. On the other side the skeletons of leafless trees began to take shape. She stepped inside the cabin but continued to watch through the partially opened door. She could see shadowy figures moving from tree to tree, and occasionally the bright flash of musket fire.

Then, through the trees, she saw the red and white uniform of a British soldier. He was waving a sword as if motioning other men to follow him. *How can this be?* she worried. *Those Kentucky soldiers chased off the British three days ago. Certainly the British reinforcements couldn't have arrived from Detroit this soon. But why are our soldiers pulling back?*

But the shadowy figures in their buckskins and tattered American uniforms *were* retreating toward her. Some had already backed out into the open meadow while the Redcoats advanced toward them through the woods.

Suddenly, up over the bank of the frozen river alongside the meadow rose a stampede of screaming Indians, waving their tomahawks and guns as they charged across the field toward the helpless Kentuckians and local settlers.

As she watched, Audry Hamilton suddenly recognized her husband retreating with the other settlers across the field . . . then, horrified, she saw him crumple to the snow under the withering blow of an Indian war club.

She slammed the door and collapsed to the floor.

Sergeant Thompson of the Kentucky militia lay sprawled in the snow, knocked unconscious by a musket ball that had grazed his head. As the afternoon sun warmed his back, he gradually became aware of the icy snow in his face, the throbbing in his head, and the chilly dampness of his uniform.

Where was he? What had happened? He tried to think, but the throbbing in his head made it difficult.

The young sergeant tried to sit up. He was stiff, but except for a monstrous headache, he didn't seem to be wounded anywhere. He looked around, wincing as he saw the bodies of fellow soldiers sprawled in snow stained red with their blood. A young man in buckskins—one of the settlers, obviously—lay dead nearby.

Now he remembered. His militia had come north from Kentucky with General Winchester to help the Michigan settlers fight off the British and their Indian allies. The fighting had gone back and forth most of 1812. The new year had already started as General Winchester and his Kentuckians had come to the aid of Frenchtown, a small village being used by the British to store supplies. But the communication had said there were only a few British soldiers and Indians—the village could be easily won back if the Americans got some help.

Thompson staggered to his feet. Something had

gone terribly wrong. From out of nowhere, hundreds of Redcoats . . . hundreds of Indians . . .

The blood circulated in his cold limbs as he trudged slowly toward the village, and he began to feel stronger. But the village itself was in chaos. Much of the flimsy stockade had been burned or knocked down. Some of the cabins had been burned or damaged by cannon fire. Wounded men—both soldiers and settlers—were propped against the remaining buildings.

The sergeant recognized one of his soldiers, a bloody bandage wrapped around his knee. "Where's General Winchester?" he demanded.

"Captured," the man said dully.

Thompson swallowed. "Why are these wounded outside? They'll freeze out here before morning."

"No room," muttered the man. "A few criticals inside . . . plus women and children."

Sergeant Thompson realized he had to do something to get these men inside. He went from cabin to cabin, trying to see if he could squeeze in a few more. He didn't have much luck in the village, but some of the families had lived outside the stockade. He'd check those out, too.

About a hundred yards south of the village, he came across a silent cabin. In the winter evening's twilight he could see that the door was torn off its leather hinges and one corner of the small dwelling was blackened. The Indians had apparently tried to set it on fire, but for some reason, the flames had gone out.

"Hello. Hello? Is anybody here?" he called as he ventured inside the house. In the shadows he could see that the furniture was broken and all the food stores had been raided. Pots, pans, blankets, and anything of value had been taken. No one was there.

"We can use this cabin for a hospital," he murmured to himself, turning back to the village to get some help to move the wounded men. But as he walked around to the back of the cabin, he was startled by a sound. At first he thought it was a kitten meowing, and he was ready to ignore it, but something made him investigate.

The whimpering sound seemed to come from a barrel sitting under the eaves of the cabin. He popped open the lid and jumped back. "Heaven help us! What have we here?" he said, looking down into the gloom of the barrel.

Staring up at him was the tear-stained face of a small boy.

"Lad? You okay? Whatcha doin' in there?"

The boy didn't answer . . . only clung to Thompson as the sergeant gently pulled him out and carried him back to the village.

Most of the settlers were too traumatized to even give the boy a glance as Thompson tried to discover who the boy was. Finally one harried woman recognized the child. "Why, that's the Hamilton boy. They live just outside the stockade."

"They don't no more," spoke up a wounded Frenchtown man. "I seen Black Hawk carrying off his mother this mornin'."

Thompson was shocked. “What do you mean, man?”

“I was lyin’ out there in the middle of the field with my legs shot out from under me when he came walking by with the boy’s mother under his arm like she was a sack of flour. But you can believe she was kickin’ and screamin’ plenty.”

“Who’s this Black Hawk?” demanded Sergeant Thompson. “How do you know it was him?”

“It was him, all right. Him and some of his braves were fightin’ alongside the British. They were the ones that took over the town before you all came. Huh! He’s big and strong as Goliath. I’d recognize him anywhere.”

“What about the boy’s pappy?” said Thompson.

“Well, now, he’s sure enough dead. His body’s right out there in the snow with the rest of ’em. God rest their souls,” muttered the settler.

As the man’s words sank in, Thompson felt the boy’s small body still clinging to him. The boy was an orphan. Who was going to take care of him?

The young Kentuckian talked to several of the Frenchtown families, but it soon became apparent the survivors were too overwhelmed to take on anything more. Many of the original thirty-three families had been completely wiped out. None had escaped the loss of some family members. It was the middle of winter, and the British and Indians were still in the area threatening further attacks.

“We just can’t take him,” said a woman who had lost her husband and whose cabin had been burned to the ground. She and her children had survived by tunneling into a haystack to hide. "I'm goin' back to Boston before we starve," she said. "It'll be hard enough with five young'uns. I couldn't possibly handle another one."

"But . . . but someone has to take him!" Sergeant Thompson sputtered.

"You're from Kentucky," noted the man who had seen the Indians carrying off Mrs. Hamilton. "His father has kinfolk there—Logan County, I think. Take the boy back with you. Let the Hamiltons raise him."

Sergeant Thompson didn't know what to do. But right then he had more immediate concerns—like getting his wounded men under cover for the night. He began gathering up those who could walk and together they carried others until thirty exhausted Kentuckians and little Gilbert were crowded into the Hamiltons' tiny cabin outside the town's stockade. They propped the door in place and lit a fire, but they were too tired to bring in enough wood to keep it going until morning.

With first light, Sergeant Thompson was awakened by someone shaking him. He turned over to see that the door had been removed. A tall, stern-looking Indian stood over him with his finger to his lips for silence. Then he motioned Thompson to follow.

Outside, Thompson heard a terrible howling and screaming coming from the village. He staggered to the corner of the cabin and saw smoke and flames billowing above the broken-down fence around the town.

"White man's firewater make Indians go crazy," explained the Indian. "You leave now or die!"

Thompson looked again. Indians were running everywhere looting the cabins, scalping the unarmed inhabitants, and burning the remaining buildings.

"We must stop them!"

"You could not stop them. You must leave!" To a military man like Thompson, it sounded like an order. Then the Indian turned to him and said, "I'm Black Hawk. They are not my braves, but I will try to stop them."

Black Hawk! Thompson was stunned. Why was he warning them? Just yesterday he was fighting on the side of the British. "Why—?" he blurted.

The big Indian's eyes narrowed. "Killing the wounded is not honorable," he said.

Thompson turned back toward the cabin door, his first impulse to rally his men and race to the village. But Black Hawk was right; there really was nothing he could do. His men were all unarmed and seriously wounded. Maybe he should just try to get them to safety.

He stopped, remembering something. "Hey, did you take a white woman from this—?" But Black Hawk was gone.

Quietly Thompson woke up his men. With some hobbling on makeshift crutches and others supporting their comrades, the party made its way across the meadow and into the woods . . . with the little Hamilton boy riding on the sergeant's shoulders.

Chapter 2

Life Without Mama

THE THRIVING HAMILTON PLANTATION in Logan County, Kentucky, had been home to Gil Hamilton for almost ten years now. At thirteen, Gil was stronger than his cousin Robbie—even though the other boy was a year older—and almost as tall. Gil's hair had turned from the sandy curls of childhood to a straight, dark brown, and his thick eyebrows shaded searching eyes. He was a good-looking boy with full lips and a strong jawline. A trace of peach fuzz had begun to show on his upper lip.

In the hustle and

bustle of a busy southern plantation, Gil found it hard to recall the details of his early childhood in a frontier cabin in Michigan. Still, he thought about it often, sitting in the crook of an old hickory tree just out of sight of the big house.

He remembered it had been cold and snowy. He remembered feeling happy when his father was home. (At least he knew what his father looked like; Uncle George had a photograph in the parlor.) He remembered being rocked gently in his mother's rocking chair and vaguely remembered that she had blue eyes and dark hair. But no matter how hard he tried, he could not recall an image of her face. In fact, the only thing he could clearly remember was that she used to sing to him. (Funny, he thought. Aunt Edith never sang.) He especially remembered his mother's lullaby about the moon.

I see the moon, and the moon sees me.
God bless the moon, and God bless me. . . .

Gil went over and over the song in his mind until he came to think of his mother as the Blue-eyed Moon Singer.

"Aunt Edith," he said late one afternoon as his aunt was doing some embroidery on the big veranda. "Don't you think there's a chance that my mama's still alive?"

Aunt Edith Hamilton rolled her eyes. "Gracious, child, haven't we been over this a dozen times? When will you ever get it through your thick head? She's most likely dead, and you're better off forgettin' about her."

"But we don't *know* that she's dead," Gil protested. "I mean, didn't that soldier who brought me here say that she got carried off by some Indian?"

"I can't remember what that ragtag soldier told us anymore. Ask your uncle—no! Just forget the whole thing."

"But why? Why forget about her?"

" 'Why? Why? Why?' All you ever do is ask why. When will you give me a little peace and quiet?"

"I don't know." Gil stared at the floor of the veranda with a discouraged look on his face. Then the line of his mouth hardened. "But I don't see why I should forget about my own mother. She wouldn't forget about me."

Too late, Gil realized his aunt was getting frustrated with his questions. With a tilt of her chin and a lift of one eyebrow she snapped, "Well, maybe she *did* forget you. Maybe that's why you haven't heard from her in all these years."

Her words cut Gil deeply. No one had ever come out and said the thing he feared most. Sometimes at night, when everything was silent and dark, he too wondered why his mother had never contacted him. Why hadn't she run away from the Indians and come back to him? Why hadn't she at least written him a letter? There were traders going among the Indians all the time. Surely she could have sent some sort of a message even if she couldn't escape.

Seeing his pain, his aunt softened. "There, there,

now. I'm sorry, Gil . . . but I'm just trying to look out for you. You pine away for her too much; it does a body no good. That's why I keep telling you it's better for us all to accept that she's no longer alive . . . at least not to us."

She patted Gil's shoulder. "Look, you're getting older now. You need to face the facts. Suppose she was still alive—why, living with Indians this long would have changed her beyond recognition. She would've become one of them by now. I've seen it happen before." Edith Hamilton laid down her embroidery and looked down the broad drive leading up to the house. "When we came here to Kentucky years ago, they rescued a little girl who had been taken by some Indians. She was just like a wild animal. She couldn't speak English and wouldn't wear proper clothes or eat at a table . . . such a shame. I don't know what happened to the poor child, but I can tell you that she was not civilizable. And . . . I'm afraid your mother would be the same way."

Gil's pain turned to anger. "You never did like my mother. You don't want her to be alive."

Aunt Edith looked shocked. "Now that's not true, Gilbert. We all mourn the loss of your parents."

"Yes, but I heard you say once that you didn't think my father should have married her."

His aunt looked flustered. "Well, he did marry below his station in life, and if he had found a nice girl around here from a more . . . well, a more *established* family, he might not have gone off to that God-forsaken Michigan territory. But—"

"You make it sound like it was all Mama's fault," Gil interrupted.

"No, no. I'm not blaming her for the war and all. But it is true that it was her idea to make a new start in that wild frontier."

Gil's face was stormy. "That's because you and all the society people around here wouldn't accept her."

"You watch your tongue, Gilbert Hamilton! There's no need to get sassy. None of us wanted to see your parents suffer. But you of all people should be grateful that you were rescued—not just from the Indians but from that rough and . . . and barbaric life. You were fortunate to be brought back here to grow up in a more refined culture."

Aunt Edith stood up. "So now," the thin-faced woman continued, taking a big breath and packing away her embroidery into its neat little bag, "I don't think we should talk about this any longer. It's too upsetting. That's why you should forget about it. The subject leads to nothin' but grief every time you bring it up. Go on, now. Find something to do with Robbie." And she marched into the house, her many skirts swishing around her.

Gil stood leaning against one of the great white columns that lined the front of the mansion. He smashed his black hat onto his head. In front of him the lawn dropped away smoothly to the stone fence. Beyond it were the tobacco fields where the slaves were hoeing the tender young plants.

"Can I get you somethin', Masta Gil?" It was one of the house Negroes who had been polishing the brass lamps on either side of the door.

"Nah, that's okay, Jubal. But do you know where Robbie is?"

"Oh, I reckon he's up with de hounds, suh."

Gil shrugged. He loved to run the hounds as much as Robbie, chasing foxes or rabbits by day or raccoons at night—it didn't make much difference. But even that sport had turned sour a few weeks earlier when he had asked Uncle George if he could have a dog of his own.

"What do you want with a hound, boy? Can't do nothin' with one dog except love it up too much an' spoil it. Now I know for a fact that Robbie's willin' to include you anytime he takes his dogs huntin'. Ain't that right, son?" Uncle George smiled at Robbie, then turned back to Gil. "There, see what I told you? You don't need no hound of your own."

Gil stared blankly at his uncle. Sure, he could run the hounds; in fact, he had the run of the whole plantation. But it was not his, and no part of it ever would be. Robbie would be the sole heir to all of Aunt Edith and Uncle George's great wealth. In subtle ways they reminded him that he was not really a part of the family. He was the orphaned cousin whose inheritance had been lost with his mother and father in the War of 1812.

Uncle George scowled as he watched the disappointment spread on Gil's face. "Now don't turn sour on me," he said. "We gave you a horse—and a fine one at that—'cause you need a way to get around. But one animal is enough to learn proper responsibility. You should be grateful and quit your mopin'."

So, Gil realized, that's the way it was going to be. Even though Aunt Edith and Uncle George were "kind" enough to raise him, that would be the end of it. Once grown, he knew he'd be on his own.

When Gil found Robbie near the kennel, his cousin was just finishing cleaning his rifle.

"Hey, Gil, you want to go coonin' tonight? The moon'll be out. Oughta be a good night for it."

"Nah. Not tonight."

Robbie looked at his cousin and wrinkled his nose like he smelled something bad. "What's the matter with you, anyway? You're in some kind of a foul mood that I don't understand. What's wrong?"

"Ain't nothin' wrong with me. I just don't feel like coonin', that's all."

Robbie thought a moment, then stood up, wiping his hands. "I got an idea," he said. "I hear the Methodists are starting their summer camp meetings tonight. That oughta be good for a laugh or two. Let's go see what's poppin'."

"What's camp meetings?" asked Gil.

"Haven't you heard? It's an outdoor revival, goes on for days."

The Hamiltons were not religious people. Uncle George said a memorized prayer each noon at dinner, and the family engaged a parson for baptizing, marrying, and burying when they or any of their slaves required it. "We're not like those sorry folks who have their slaves 'jump the broom' when they want to get married," explained Aunt Edith. "We do them proper, with a preacher." But apart from that, the Hamiltons had very little to do with church.

Seeing that Gil hadn't heard anything about camp meetings, Robbie continued. "You know, they're like church services: singin', preachin', and all that. I hear these Methodists really whoop it up sometimes. They shout and they dance around, and sometimes they fall down on the ground and get the jerks," said Robbie. Seeing the bewildered look on Gil's face, he moaned loudly, "Help me, Gil! I think I'm gettin' them right now." The older boy fell to the ground, rolled his eyes, let his tongue hang out, then began shaking and twitching all over.

Thinking that Robbie was having some kind of a fit, Gil grabbed the dogs' water bucket and, quick as greased lightning, threw it on his cousin.

Robbie jumped to his feet coughing and sputtering. "What'd ya go and do that for?" he yelled. "I didn't need no revivin'. I was just tryin' to show you what the jerks look like."

"Oh. You seen 'em before?" asked Gil, his eyes wide with wonder.

"No! I ain't never seen 'em. But I heard tell." He tried to brush himself off, but his dirty hands just made muddy smears. "Now look at what a mess you made. I got mud all over me. I'm gonna have to go change before dinner."

"Sorry, Robbie." Then after a minute Gil added,

"Where'd you say they're havin' those meetings?"

"I didn't say, but they're supposed to be down in that meadow near Swope's mill." He watched Gil for a moment then added, "Well, you wanna go tonight or not?"

Chapter 3

The Big Camp Meetin'

THE BOYS ARRIVED at the Methodist camp meeting just before sunset.

Wagons and carriages were parked all around the edge of a large meadow where families camped with little cooking fires and tents for sleeping. More campsites extended as far off into the woods as Gil could see.

At one end of the field a large platform had been built about chest high. Above it, supported by poles, was a simple shake-covered roof. Several chairs sat on the platform, and at the front was a pulpit. "That must be the preacher's stand," said Gil.

Extending out in front of the platform were row upon row of split-log benches. Robbie looked around in amazement. "I never thought there would be this many people. There must be five hundred people."

"And there're still more coming." Gil pointed to some carriages that were just arriving filled with finely dressed people. "Hey, aren't those the Adams brothers from the plantation over the hill from us?"

"Yeah, and look who they got with them." Robbie whistled softly at two young ladies dressed in fine silks. One had her hair all done up with jeweled combs. The other wore a fancy hat with feathers.

Most of the families who had arrived earlier were finishing their evening meal at their campsites. "I don't recognize many of the campers," said Robbie.

"That's probably because they came from far away," said Gil.

"Could be. I reckon they're mostly Methodists. Most of them dress in plain clothes with no jewelry or ruffles."

"Yeah, but they don't seem very religious," said Gil. "They're laughin' and greetin' each other like they are at a family reunion."

"Who said religious people have to be down in the mouth? They just ain't so rowdy as some of these others."

It was true that many of the fancily dressed newcomers acted more like they were at some kind of a sporting event, slapping each other on the back and pointing. Gil noticed that when the Adams brothers went over to a knot of these more boisterous men, a flask of whiskey was passed around.

"You can tell they ain't Methodists," Robbie snorted as they walked past the group. "Methodists don't drink."

A bluish haze from campfire smoke drifted lazily over the meeting grounds, giving the summer evening a festive feel. Crickets chirped warmly, and bats were on the wing to get the mosquitoes before they got the people.

Finally a trumpet sounded, and the people began to move toward the benches while two men lit lanterns suspended from the roof of the preachers' platform and from poles set in the ground among the log seats.

The more plainly dressed people divided themselves, men on the left and ladies on the right. Slowly, the others saw what was happening, and they did likewise.

Robbie and Gil found seats about halfway back near the center aisle. Just across from them sat the fancy women who had come with the Adams brothers.

Several men took their seats on the platform, and one square-faced, solidly built man in a black suit stood up and began to sing a hymn. The Methodists, or at least those campers Gil and Robbie assumed were Methodists, stood up and joined in. The fancy visitors sat or stood as they pleased.

"That must be Peter Cartwright," whispered Robbie, indicating the singer. "He's the main preacher. I hear he lives over in Christian County, but he travels all over the country preachin'."

After singing several songs, Peter Cartwright began to preach. Gil didn't pay much attention to what was being said. He wanted to know if anyone would get the jerks or do anything else unusual. So he kept watching the people around him.

Peter Cartwright preached on and on telling people to repent of their sins and be converted to Christ. In time, Gil began to sense a change in the crowd. He could hear people softly weeping. Some walked forward to kneel down near the platform, and Peter Cartwright called for some "mourners" (counselors) to come pray with the seekers. Some of the seekers were crying out for Jesus to forgive them.

Right across the aisle from him, Gill noticed that the two women who had come with the Adams brothers were whispering and laughing and pointing at some of the people who had gone forward. Then, suddenly, they let out a great cry. They raised their hands and began to shake, not just a little bit like Robbie had that morning on the ground near the kennel. These women's heads and arms were snapping back and forth like whips. The hat flew off the one, and the jeweled combs came out of the hair of the other. Their faces got red, and they seemed terribly embarrassed as they cried for it to stop.

The Adams brothers climbed over the benches and ran to the aid of their ladies, but they were helpless to stop the jerks.

By this time the whole congregation was watching, except for some of the regular Methodists who had begun to sing a hymn and pray.

The jerks continued for several minutes until the two ladies were in a total disarray, hair flying everywhere. Finally, they both fainted, and the jerking stopped. The Adams brothers eased them gently onto their bench, and in a few moments the women came to, saying they were fine and just needed a drink of water. The brothers took them out.

People were still praying at the front when Peter Cartwright closed the service and came walking down the aisle toward the back.

"I gotta go meet someone," Robbie said. "It won't take long, so don't leave without me." And he turned to fight his way through the crowd.

As his cousin left, Gil shrugged and moved along behind Peter Cartwright with all the rest of the people who where leaving the seating area. Cartwright was busy shaking hands and greeting people. Then the preacher excused himself and headed off toward the trees. Curious, Gil followed along and was surprised to see the Adams brothers waiting under a lantern at the edge of the woods. They both had horsewhips in their hands and were looking right at the preacher.

"Are you looking for me?" called Cartwright to the brothers.

"That we are," the older one responded angrily. "We're going to teach you never to give anyone the jerks again."

Cartwright's pace didn't slow a bit as he walked toward them. "Let me tell you boys somethin'. I don't give no one the jerks. I don't even think they're a

good thing. But sometimes they come on people—righteous or sinner alike—and they can't help it. So don't blame me." He stopped about twenty feet away and turned as if he were intending to make off in another direction.

"Ha!" the other Adams brother said, stepping forward and snaking the whip out in front of him until it gave a little snap. "We know you did it, and you're not gonna get out of what's coming to you that easily."

Cartwright turned back toward the men. "Well, I'm telling you the truth. I had nothin' to do with it." He started closing the distance between them. "But if you think differently, then you better look out, 'cause whatever I can do, I'm gonna do to you." He pointed his finger right at them as he walked toward them.

"Now hold on there! You ain't got no cause for that," the brothers said as they both backed up.

But Cartwright kept marching. He was clearly in range of their whips by then, but the Adams boys kept backing up until one of them tripped over a stone; then they both turned and ran off into the dark.

Later, as they walked home in the pale light of the first quarter moon, Gil told Robbie about Cartwright and the Adams boys.

"You think he'd have given them the jerks?" asked Robbie.

"All I know is what I told ya, and he said he had nothin' to do with them jerks. Personally, I just think he's not a back-down man. I think he'd have kept comin' at them boys even if they were flickin' lice off him with those whips. That's what I think."

"Well, if that don't beat all," mused Robbie. "Hey, wanna come back tomorrow night? I met some girls—real pretty ones, too. One of them was Cartwright's daughter. Her name's Eliza." He grinned in the moonlight. "Even found out where she lives—two miles this side of Hopkinsville, just off the road between here and there. We could ride on over and see her some time."

Gil shrugged. "That's a long ride—over fifteen miles." Then he grinned. His cousin was always scheming something.

The next night the boys arrived at the meeting grounds a little earlier. Robbie and Gil were quick to locate where the young people were gathering on the small bridge over the stream that fed Swope's pond.

Robbie punched Gil in the side with his elbow. "There, that younger one with the long black hair. That's Eliza Cartwright. Ain't she somethin'? I'm gonna sit near her tonight." Eliza and some of the other girls were throwing bread crumbs to some eager ducks in the water below.

When the trumpet sounded for the meeting to begin, Robbie made good on his plan to sit near Eliza. In fact, with his encouragement, all the boys filed into the row right behind the girls. Gil followed along, too. There was lots of giggling by the girls and jokes among the boys.

It didn't take long for Peter Cartwright to notice that a whole row of boys was sitting on the ladies' side of the congregation. When he got up to preach, he said, "I'd like all the *gentlemen* to move from the ladies' section." When no one immediately moved, he continued. "That way we will be able to see how many country clowns and town fools there are, for of course they won't move!"

Nervous snickering and whispering spread throughout the congregation, and Gil and several of the other boys got up and moved to the other side as quickly as possible, finding seats where they could.

Gil thought all the boys had moved, but when he looked back, Robbie, who had been sitting near the far end of the row from him, and a couple other boys had remained where they were. They were ducking their heads down to be as inconspicuous as possible.

But that didn't fool Peter Cartwright. He cleared his throat and with a booming voice said, "Thank you, *gentlemen*. Now let's see how many *clowns* we have." He pointed toward the wayward boys and said, "I see one right there on the end of the . . . let's see, what is it . . . yes, the tenth row. Would you please stand up. Yes, you young man, you in the brown jacket. Stand up there and take a bow."

Robbie, unable to remain concealed any longer, sheepishly came to his feet.

"What's the matter, young man? Are you not able to tell the difference between the gentlemen and the ladies in this crowd? It seems pretty easy to me. The ladies are the ones wearing the dresses. Now you wouldn't be hiding a dress under those long pants of yours, would you?"

The crowd roared with laughter, especially the girls in row nine.

Robbie's neck and cheeks became bright red, and he turned and ran for the back. The other boys followed, stooping over like they were trying to hide behind a hedge. The crowd laughed all the louder.

When things had quieted down, Peter Cartwright began his sermon. This time Gil listened more closely, forgetting about Robbie as Cartwright preached about the Good Shepherd leaving ninety-nine sheep in the fold to find one lost sheep.

As he listened, a familiar, lonely feeling squeezed Gil's insides. He often felt like a lost sheep without a home.

When the sermon ended, the congregation stood and sang an old Charles Wesley song:

How happy every child of grace,
Who knows his sins forgiven!
"This earth," he cries, "is not my place,
I seek my place in heaven."

After the meeting, Gil couldn't find Robbie anywhere, so he walked home alone, humming to himself the wistful tune of the final song. *Huh,* thought Gil, *one thing is for sure: The Hamilton plantation is not my place.*

Chapter 4

The Cornstalk Duel

WHEN GIL CAME DOWN for breakfast the next morning, George Hamilton was ranting and raving to his wife that no preacher had the right to make fun of a Hamilton. Gil glanced at his cousin. Robbie must have already told his father about what happened at the camp meeting—probably as soon as he got home the night before.

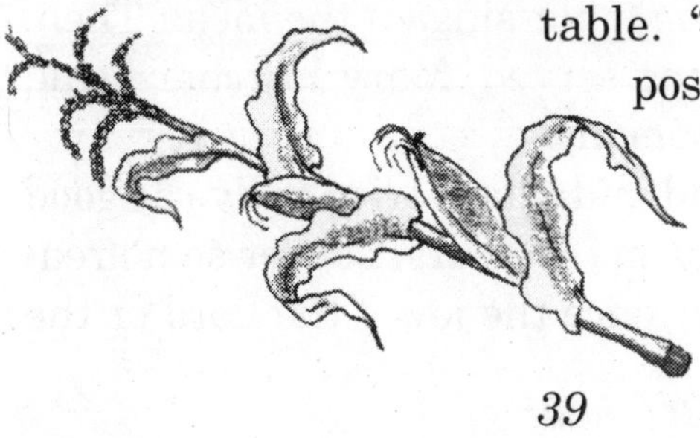

"And I'm gonna put it straight to him," Uncle George fumed to the family at the breakfast table. "I heard he's supposed to be having dinner over at the Pritchards' this noon, and I aim to be there. Pritchard bought those oxen from me, and this seems like the perfect time to deliver them." Gil knew that if his uncle was at the Pritchards anywhere near mealtime, Kentucky hospitality required that he be invited to join the table. "You boys want to come along?" his uncle said smugly.

"Sure," Gil said, but Robbie only shrugged and drew faces in the egg yolk that still smeared his plate.

At midmorning when it was time to leave for the Pritchards, Robbie wasn't anywhere to be found. "Where is that boy?" complained Gil's uncle after waiting for ten minutes. "We better leave without him, Gilbert."

George Hamilton was right about the Pritchards' hospitality. He and Gil were invited to dinner. But they were not the only guests. The Pritchards had invited several other neighbors who were interested in the camp meetings to enjoy a visit with the famous traveling preacher from Hopkinsville. Fourteen were seated around the table.

Wilbur Pritchard invited Peter Cartwright to honor them by asking a blessing on the meal. Then, as the meal was being served, Mary Pritchard said she had an announcement.

"My dear husband and I have tried to live as good Christians should for many years, but for some reason I could not experience the joy of the Lord or the sense of His perfect love," the mistress of the house began shyly. "Then last night at the meeting, I went forward and prayed for these blessings—oh, please start eating," she said, noticing that everyone was politely waiting for her. "The food will get cold."

The guests gratefully dug into the fried chicken and sweet potatoes.

"While I was praying last night," continued Mary Pritchard, "many others received the gift of joy, but something stood in my way. And then Brother Cartwright came by to pray with me." She paused and looked at the preacher, who was paying particular attention to a chicken leg. "He asked if there were any people whom I was not treating with the kind of love I desired to experience from God. Suddenly, before my mind's eye marched a whole line of people—"

"Well, it was none of us, I'm sure, Mary," injected the woman across the table. "You are much too kind."

"No," continued Mrs. Pritchard, "it included none of you. It was a parade of our slaves. The Lord seemed to say, 'How can you ask a greater blessing of love from Me while you hold your fellow human beings in bondage?' For the first time, I could clearly see my sin. Right there and then I promised the Lord that we would free our slaves."

A cry of surprise went up around the table, and some of the women put their hands over their mouths, totally shocked. Gil noticed that his uncle had stopped eating, and a deep frown covered his face.

"And what's more," continued Mrs. Pritchard, "no sooner had I made this promise to God than I felt an overwhelming sense of His love. I rose from my knees and began singing and praising the Lord. You saw me, didn't you, Nancy May?"

"Why, indeed I did. You were fairly dancin' and shoutin', but I had no idea—"

"Of course you didn't, and that's the reason we've invited you all here today. We wanted to tell you personally, as our nearest neighbors . . . before tonight's meeting."

" 'We?' " questioned an older man with white whiskers and wide eyes. "Certainly you both aren't in on this foolishness, are you? What about it, Wilbur? You've always been a reasonable man."

Wilbur Pritchard cleared his throat. "I most certainly am in on it. In fact—"

"This is—it's crazy," interrupted George Hamilton. "You'll stir up unrest on every plantation for miles around. You can't do this!"

Before either of the Pritchards could reply, Hamilton leaned toward his host. "Listen to me, Wilbur Pritchard. Don't let this crazy preacher destroy you. Think about it! How will you run your plantation?"

"I . . . don't really know yet," their host said honestly. "We'll manage somehow. I'm sure the Lord will provide. But let me say it again so you all understand very clearly. I agree completely with my wife. For some time, I've felt it's not right to treat other people as property. So we will be granting our slaves their rightful freedom."

"Well, you don't intend to do it right away, do you?" put in another neighbor. "Maybe you could make it part of your will or something so that when you die, they'll be free. I've heard of people doing that before. I mean, as the Bible says, 'Let all things be done decently and in order.' "

"If you're going to bring the Bible into this," inserted Peter Cartwright, "you better ask whether you would like to wait twenty or twenty-five years for your freedom. That's not what Paul had in mind when he said to do things 'decently and in order.' "

"But you can't just turn all those colored people out to run around begging from the rest of us," protested another neighbor. "What are they gonna do?"

Wilbur Pritchard wiped his mustache. "We'll be glad to employ any of them who wish to stay here—"

"You mean actually pay them?" said one woman in disbelief.

"Yes, whatever's fair. But the point is, they'll be free to go. We intend to take them all to the meeting tonight and give them their papers there. That's 'decently and in order' enough as far as I can see," he said.

"Gentlemen and ladies," said a flabbergasted George Hamilton, spreading his hands out in an appeal for reason. "I think it's time for all of us to see how outrageous this preacher is and reject the foolish ideas he's planting in our midst. His only purpose is to stir up trouble. Just last night, when a few boys innocently sat on the women's side of the congregation, he insulted them publicly. Now, there's no call for that kind of thing. He's just a rabble-rouser."

Cartwright cleared his throat. "Were you at the meeting last night, Mr. Hamilton?"

"No I wasn't, but I expect by now everyone has heard the story."

"Possibly they have, Mr. Hamilton, but I hope not with the twist you're putting on it."

"What do you mean?"

"Let me put it this way: If a company of Shawnee Indians, who know nothing of our customs, were to come into one of our religious meetings and see all the women seated on one side and the men on the other, they would have manners enough to take their seats accordingly."

Gil looked down in embarrassment, thinking about where he had sat. He hadn't meant any disrespect, but he could now see that it wasn't very courteous.

George Hamilton cleared his throat and looked around at the other guests. "No, I disagree. I believe Indians would have sat just where they wanted," he said. Gil noticed that he rose taller in his seat in what looked like a self-righteous pose.

"Well," said Cartwright firmly, "it's my opinion that they would, so I think they must have more manners than those disruptive young men last night. If they can't respond to a gentle rebuke and do what's right, then bringing a little shame on their heads is exactly what they were asking for. I gave 'em fair warning. They just had no manners."

"Now you've gone too far! How dare you say my son is less of a gentleman than the savages! If there weren't ladies here, I would call you out right now."

Gil looked at his uncle in shock. Was he threatening to fight Peter Cartwright?

"If you are trying to frighten me, Mr. Hamilton," said Cartwright, "you won't get very far. I intend to do my duty in keeping order in the congregation as is *my* business, and you'd do as well to mind *your* business."

George Hamilton's ears grew red. "Why, you yellow-bellied scoundrel. You're just hiding behind your preacher's cloak."

"That I'm not. But you'd better be careful, Mr. Hamilton. I was quite a boxer in my day, and if the devil should get out of you and into me, I might give you the whipping of your life."

"You think so, do you?" spat George Hamilton as he stood up, nearly knocking over his chair. He threw down his napkin and raged, "If I thought you weren't such a coward, I would challenge you to a duel."

Peter Cartwright took another bite of biscuit and then, without looking up, said very calmly, "Well, sir, if you challenge me, I will accept."

"Then I do," roared George Hamilton. "Right here and now, I challenge you to mortal combat."

The whole room became silent. Not one fork moved. No one chewed—except Peter Cartwright. Everyone was staring at the two men, one standing and roaring his challenge, the other sitting, calmly

continuing his meal.

Finally Peter Cartwright looked up. "Very well,

sir. I'll fight you if you insist. However, there's just one matter. Is it not true that according to the laws of honor, since you challenged me, it is my right to choose the weapons with which we are to fight?"

"Absolutely. Make your choice. What'll it be? Pistols? Swords?"

"Oh, no, not right here on our plantation!" cried Mrs. Pritchard.

"Well, then," said Cartwright, still as calm as could be, "let's step outside and go into that field we can see through the window, get a couple young cornstalks, and have at it with 'em. I think that ought to settle things quite well enough. Don't you?" And he smiled broadly with his big, crooked grin.

George Hamilton's face tightened; his eyes bulged, and he began working his jaw so that his long sideburns pulsed. He clinched and raised his fists. But no one was watching him. They were staring in astonishment at Peter Cartwright.

Then Mrs. Pritchard began to laugh, and soon everyone joined in as they all realized how the Methodist preacher had demonstrated the foolishness of fighting over such things.

But George Hamilton did not laugh. While the others were holding their sides with laughter or clapping in amusement, Gil's uncle marched angrily out of the room.

Chapter 5

Free for All

GIL WASN'T SURE HIS UNCLE would give him permission to attend that evening's camp meeting, so he went to the camp grounds without even asking. It was the last night, and Gil's curiosity was high. Would the Pritchards really release their slaves?

True to their word, the Pritchards brought all their slaves—nineteen men, women, and children. Even though they sat near the back with the men and women on the appropriate sides, their arrival caused a great stir as other people in the congregation turned around to look. It wasn't that black people never attended the meetings; Peter Cartwright made it clear that both free and slave were welcome in his meetings. But those who attended were usually drivers or servants for the white people. Occasionally a few free blacks came and stood near the back in ones or twos.

The arrival of what was obviously a plantation's whole black population, however, was truly a curiosity. Whispers passed up and down the rows as people speculated about the reason for their presence.

Cartwright wasted no time in enlightening them. "Mr. and Mrs. Pritchard," he announced from the speakers' platform, "I understand you have a testimony about the Lord's goodness. Would you like to come forward now?"

The Pritchards stood up and walked down to the speakers' platform, then looked up at Cartwright. He gave them an encouraging smile. The Pritchards turned around, and then Wilbur called out the name of each slave and instructed them to all come forward and stand in a line facing the congregation.

Gil was certain the blacks had no idea why they were being called forward. Parents clutched their children tightly and looked at one another with worried eyes. Hesitantly, they all came to the front.

Without saying a word, the Pritchards went down the line and gave each person a sheet of paper. Most, obviously, couldn't read, but a few figured out enough of the words to get an idea of what the paper said. Mouths dropped open, tears rolled down cheeks, and faces glowed with such surprise and awe that Gil thought some were going to faint.

"In obedience to what we believe God is telling

us," shouted Wilbur Pritchard so all could hear, "we are returning your freedom to you. I say 'return' because it is not ours to give, and it certainly wasn't ours to take away. These papers have each been signed by Judge Bellingham, and they are completely legal. You are welcome to stay on the plantation and work for us for pay if you wish, or you can go where you like. From this moment on, you are free. May God bless you."

Several of the blacks fell to their knees and cried out, "Oh lordy . . . oh lordy, can this be true?" The congregation was in an uproar, some leaping to their feet and shouting at the Pritchards and Peter Cartwright, some just talking in shocked surprised to one other.

Finally Cartwright and some of the other leaders got everyone back to their seats and started a hymn to get everyone settled down. Then Peter launched into his sermon. He took John 8:36 for his text: "If the Son therefore shall make you free, ye shall be free indeed."

"Jesus was speaking of freedom from sin," he said as he gestured freely with his arms, "and that is exactly what happened here today. It was human sin that led to the enslavement of these people. But when Jesus set them free by convicting the hearts of Brother and Sister Pritchard, the Pritchards got free, too."

Gil had never heard slavery called sin before. After all, a lot of "good" Christians in Kentucky seemed to own a few slaves. But Gil could see how it

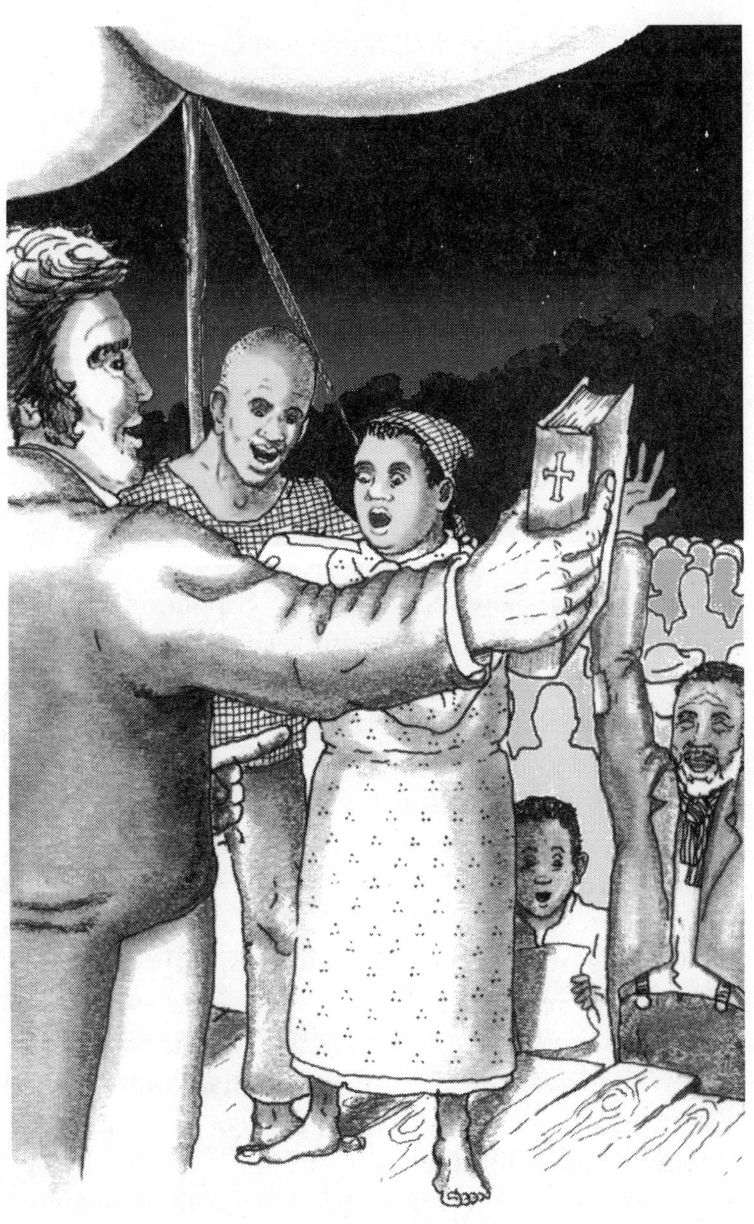

was true—Slavery just didn't seem right. But just when Gil smugly decided he agreed with Peter Cartwright, the preacher started talking about how all the people were slaves to sin whether they owned slaves or were slaves or were former slaves. "You people who got your freedom papers today can go where you wish and do what you want, but there's a greater freedom than that. All of us need to repent and seek that freedom from sin through Jesus."

When he finished preaching, Cartwright invited anyone who wanted the freedom that Jesus offers to come to the front for prayer. Many people gathered in front of the platform, including a few of the Pritchards' former slaves.

Almost without realizing it, Gil found himself walking forward, too. He didn't even know what he was feeling inside. He felt mixed up, lonely, and lost—he wanted to be "found." He tried to pray but sobs came out instead of words.

After a while, Peter Cartwright, who had been going from seeker to seeker, put his hand on Gil's shoulder and asked, "Tell me, son, what sin has brought you so much grief?"

Gil had no idea how to answer. Finally he caught his breath and said, "It's not that. I know I'm not perfect, but . . . mostly I just miss my family."

"Well, that's not a sin, boy. What happened to them?" He knew that Gil was George Hamilton's nephew, but he hadn't heard the story of why the boy was living with his uncle. So, with a little coaxing, Gil explained how he had lost his mother and father.

"Hmm," said Cartwright thoughtfully. "There are many who have lost loved ones, and I don't want to make light of your sadness in that regard, but there *is* something more precious than an earthly mother or father—and that's knowing your Heavenly Father and being assured of a place with Him."

"Yeah, I know," said Gil sadly, "but right now I just wish I knew where my mother is."

Cartwright didn't push. "Well, in time, I believe you will discover just how important your Heavenly Father is," he murmured, as if to himself. Then he said, "Have you ever tried to track down your mother?"

"No," said Gil, startled. "I wouldn't know where to start. My aunt and uncle refuse to talk about Mama, and . . . I don't think they know very much about the war anyway."

"Well, I know someone who knows everything about that war," said Peter. "A friend of mine—General Andrew Jackson. I figure he'd know that Black Hawk fellow . . . if indeed he took your mama. Fact is, Jackson would probably know where to find him, too."

"You think so?"

"I reckon so. He knows all about Indians, but . . . the War of 1812 was years ago. Black Hawk might be dead by now."

Cartwright stood up. "Say, now," the preacher said, stroking his chin as though he had a beard, "I'm fixin' to visit Jackson down at his Hermitage in Tennessee next week. You wanna go along? I'd be glad for the company."

Gil could hardly believe Peter Cartwright was taking the idea of searching for his mother seriously. As he walked back to the Hamilton plantation alone, a large full moon rose through the trees, its golden light flickering between the leaves. When it broke free to bathe the whole landscape in its soft light, a smile played with the corners of his mouth. He softly hummed and then began to sing . . .

I see the moon, and the moon sees me.
God bless the moon, and God bless me.
There's grace in the cabin
And grace in the hall,
And the grace of God is over us all.

Chapter 6

Old Hickory

At first George Hamilton was totally against Gil taking a trip with the traveling preacher. "That man is full of poppycock!" he fumed, still smarting from Cartwright's dueling joke.

But to Gil's surprise, Aunt Edith was in favor of the plan. "The boy needs to see the world and get his mind on something other than this plantation. I keep telling you, George, there's nothing here for him, and the sooner he accepts that, the better." She said it right in front of Gil, and if he hadn't been so eager to go, the words would have hurt deeply.

As it was, he felt nothing but joy when his uncle finally caved in and agreed to the plan.

Gil decided not to mention that the purpose of Cartwright's trip involved the slavery issue. Cartwright had told him that, up until that time, it had been against the rule book of the Methodist Episcopal Church for preachers to own slaves. In fact, many preached against slavery as a serious sin equal to drunkenness and gambling. "But there's a lot of people who want to change the rules," Cartwright said grimly. "They're havin' a meetin' in Nashville, Tennessee—not far from where Andrew Jackson lives—to decide the matter. And it's my intention to attend the meeting and make sure the standards don't slip!"

It was nearly noon by the time Cartwright arrived from Hopkinsville to pick up Gil. Gil rode the sleek little mare Uncle George had given him while Cartwright rode a big ugly bay. But Cartwright's horse was a fast walker with long legs and a smooth rolling gate. The stocky man leaned slightly back in the saddle so that he appeared to glide along like he was riding a sleigh on snow.

"You think that pony of yours can keep up?" he asked Gil as they turned onto the road to Nashville.

"Sure," Gil said. Knowing the older man had already ridden fifteen miles, Gil was sure Cartwright couldn't keep up the brisk pace for long. "Before we get out of Logan County, you won't even smell my dust." But Gil was already having to spur his little mare into a trot from time to time just to keep up.

"When I was your age," chuckled the preacher, "I raced horses and was a considerable gambler 'til I got converted. I don't doubt your mount could go like the wind from here to yonder." He thrust his square chin toward the tree line on the far side of a long meadow. "But the question is, will she fade before day's end?"

Gil smiled to himself, thinking that he'd show the preacher. But when the afternoon shadows had lengthened, the man's horse had not slowed a trifle, while Gil's mare was nearly tuckered out. As they came down a rise where the road crossed a stream, they met a man riding up the wash. He wore buckskins and a big, tan floppy hat and rode bareback.

"Good day, friend," said Cartwright. "Do you know of an inn up the road where two tired travelers might get some quiet rest?"

"No, sir," drawled the man, "there's nothing along this road for many a mile, but if you're willin' to turn off the road a mile or so, there's a fine God-fearin' family that takes in strangers. I'm goin' there myself for a preachin' service . . . one of the mountain flocks I ride round to."

Delighted to meet a fellow minister, Cartwright agreed to go with the man. The three riders soon came to a poor but neat house set so tightly back into one of the many "hollers" that, if they hadn't been following the trail, they could have been within fifty yards and missed it.

Already several neighbors had gathered, and in time a small congregation of about twenty were crowded into the cabin. The mountain minister invited Peter Cartwright to preach first, and as he did so, Gil noticed that although the people listened carefully and smiled and nodded their heads in agreement, no one seemed to be affected by what Cartwright said.

When he finished, the mountain preacher rose and began singing quietly, tapping his foot, and softly clapping his hands. Soon the people joined in, and the singing got louder and faster. Every now and then the buckskin-clad preacher shouted at the top of his lungs, "Pray, brethren! Pray!" In a few minutes, the house was in an uproar that lasted for more than two hours.

When Gil and Peter Cartwright finally settled onto a pile of sweet-smelling straw in the small barn, Cartwright admitted, "It's not often I've been outpreached by nothin' but singin', clappin', and stampin', but tonight I'm satisfied to let that mountain man best me so we can get a little sleep. Man!" he whistled softly. "They could've carried on all night."

The next day the Kentucky travelers thanked their hosts and headed on toward Nashville, taking a shortcut that avoided the city itself. "We'll be back to sin city soon enough—gotta attend that church meetin'," Cartwright said. "But today I aim to get to the Hermitage, so we don't have time to gawk. Besides, ain't nothin' in Nashville to edify a man, anyway."

As they rode up the long drive to the Hermitage that afternoon, Gil was surprised that General Jackson's beautiful Tennessee plantation was larger even than his uncle's. "I thought you came here to get General Jackson's help to defeat those preachers who want to be slave owners," Gil said, as they rode between fields of slaves cutting hay. "Looks to me like he owns more slaves than everyone in Logan County put together."

"That may be true," said Cartwright, "and he knows I disapprove. But he's a good lawyer, and if he'll advise me how to defeat the spread of slavery in the church, it will be the best counsel I can get."

They were admitted to the large house by a finely dressed slave. It was not long before the general came down the stairs.

Andrew Jackson stood head and shoulders taller than the stocky Peter Cartwright, and his face was chisel sharp, topped by unruly white hair that stood mostly straight up. He had earned the name Old Hickory because of his toughness in battle, but Gil thought the name fit the way his face looked, too.

Still, Jackson welcomed them warmly as he ushered them into the parlor. "Reverend Cartwright! The last time I saw you was in Blackbourn's church in Nashville. I think you told me at the time that if I didn't get my soul converted, God would send me to hell as quick as any heathen. Am I right?"

"Yes," Cartwright smiled, then added, "and seeing all those slaves out there, I see you haven't converted yet, either. Nevertheless, I've come for your help. I need some legal advice."

"By all means," Jackson said graciously, urging them to sit on the finely upholstered chairs and sending for something cool to drink.

As Gil sipped his cold lemonade, Cartwright explained the problem. The increasing number of slave-holding preachers were trying to use the civil law to do away with the church rule against slavery. After asking a few more questions, Jackson gave Cartwright some tips on how to approach the matter in the conference meeting. Then he said, "Don't worry about how many of those preachers want to change the rule. As I always say, 'One man with courage makes a majority.' "

He stood up. "Now if you'll excuse me, I have a great deal of work to do. I don't know if you've got wind of this up there in Kentucky, but I've accepted a seat in the United States Senate, and I'm considering running for the presidency next year."

"The presidency?" said Peter Cartwright as he rose.

"Yes, sir. I think it's time for the common people to have a voice in the government of this country. We've had enough of those northern aristocrats, so I aim to give the working man a voice."

Gil looked around the plushly furnished parlor. Old Hickory's style of life was not all that far from

aristocratic itself. But Gil's fear at the moment was that the busy general was going to dismiss them before Cartwright had a chance to ask about Black

Hawk. Gil cleared his throat loudly, hoping to catch the preacher's attention, but the two men ignored him as they moved slowly toward the door.

"It's been good to see you again, Reverend. I hope everything goes well at your meeting. Solomon can show you out."

As Jackson turned away, Peter Cartwright said, "Oh. If we could trouble you for one more moment, General."

Old Hickory turned back with a this-better-be-necessary look flashing in his eyes. "Yes?"

"Well, this young man," Cartwright said, indicating Gil, "lost his parents in the War of 1812. He thinks his mother may have been kidnapped by an Indian who fought for the British."

"Oh, really?" The general turned and stared at Gil as if it were the first time he had really seen him. "Where'd this happen, son?"

Gil explained what he knew about where his family lived in southern Michigan and how he'd been saved.

The general interrupted him. "Yes. That would have been the Battle of Frenchtown on River Raisin—a nasty mess."

"I think the Indian who took my mother was called Black Hawk," said Gil. "Do you know anything about him?"

"Black Hawk! Of course. He was a Sauk, a proud leader of an honorable people. Hmm . . . he returned home to his village shortly after that, as I recall." He turned to Cartwright. "The foolish British wouldn't let the Indians collect any plunder from the battles. Fortunate for us . . . but ignorant of Indian ways of fighting."

Gil leaned forward to get the general's attention again. "But . . . do you think he took my mother?"

"I wouldn't know. It's possible—happens quite often. But then maybe it wasn't Black Hawk who took her. Could've been one of his braves."

"How can I find out?" asked Gil anxiously.

"Guess you'll have to go ask him."

"Ask! But how? Where is he?"

"In Illinois, son, Illinois . . . hmm, northwestern part, along the Mississippi, as I recall."

Chapter 7

Flirtin' and Sparkin'

GIL TRIED TO FOLLOW THE ARGUMENTS about whether or not ministers in the church should be allowed to own slaves, but the issues were complicated. Some preachers had inherited slaves or estates that were most easily run with the help of slaves. They would lose financially if they had to free the blacks.

Some of them had even hired a lawyer to show that it was illegal in the state of Tennessee to free slaves if they didn't have the means to support themselves afterward. Confronting that argument was where Andrew Jackson's advice was most helpful.

"All you have to do

to legally free them," Cartwright said to the assembled conference delegates, "is promise that you'll give them work if they need it. What's wrong with that? Just pay them a fair wage!" But he knew the real reason they wanted to keep their slaves was because it was a form of wealth. "You better not forget Jesus' warning!" he shouted. " 'It is easier for a camel to go through the eye of a needle, than for a rich man to enter into the kingdom of God.' "

In the end, the prohibition against slavery in the church was upheld, but Cartwright left the conference still troubled. "It's true that we won," he answered when Gil asked him what was the matter. "We won because there are still more of us who oppose slavery than are for it, but I didn't change many minds. It's a creeping evil. The more you see of it, the more normal it seems. I'm afraid the day will come when we can't hold the line against it in the church. What's worse, I'm afraid that someday it's gonna split this country right down the middle."

But Gil's spirit on the ride home was just as high as Cartwright's was low. For the first time in his life, he felt hope of finding his mother. But how could he get to Illinois? And if he did find Black Hawk, would the Indian know anything about his mother? What if she had died?

It's better to know than not know, he told himself as they rode back to Kentucky. *I can't keep livin' not even knowin' whether my own mother is alive or dead.*

He imagined his mother running to him across a

field with her arms open wide. But . . . what would she be like after living among the Sauks for eleven years? Would she remember him? Did she still care about him? Maybe his memories and dreams were better than the truth. After all, life with the Hamiltons was pretty good even though he knew he wouldn't inherit anything. He could learn a trade. Maybe he should leave well enough alone.

Gil was excited and terrified at the same time.

When Gil got home after being gone for almost two weeks, Robbie pulled him aside and said, "Guess what, while you were down in the big city of Nashville, I've been sparkin'."

Gil searched his cousin's face. "Oh, come on. You ain't been sparkin' with no one."

"Sure I have! I even gave her a kiss!"

"Gave *who* a kiss?"

"That Cartwright girl, Eliza. Remember, the pretty one at the camp meetin'?"

Gil frowned skeptically. "She wouldn't let you kiss her. Where'd you see her, anyway?"

"Just rode over there. Been there twice since you left. Fifteen miles ain't *that* far."

Gil didn't know whether to believe Robbie or not. Robbie was always pulling his leg with some joke or another, but from the excitement in his cousin's eyes, Gil figured something had happened. "Well, maybe you went over there, but I don't believe you kissed her. She wouldn't let you. You'd have to hold a sprig of mistletoe over her head and steal a kiss, like at Christmas."

"Well, she didn't chase me off. I'm tellin' you, Gil, she's got her cap set for me; that's for sure."

"Whaddya mean? She's no older than me."

"So what? I can wait. Besides, Martha Hopkins got married before she even turned sixteen. A couple years wouldn't be so long to wait. You come with me this afternoon, and I'll show you she's sweet on me."

Gil and Robbie rode off right after dinner. They arrived at the Cartwright place in the middle of the afternoon.

Two small boys close in age—maybe five or six—were playing in the limbs of a huge chestnut tree in front of the gray, unpainted, clapboard house when Gil and Robbie rode up. From a stout limb of the tree hung a swing with a board seat. Any grass that might have grown on the hard-packed dirt of the yard had been worn away long ago.

A girl of about eight peeked around the corner of the house and gave a shy, toothless grin, then ran out of sight, calling, " 'Liza! 'Liza! Guess who's here?"

"See, I told ya," bragged Robbie as he swung off his horse. Gil got down too and stood there holding the reins of his horse, feeling out of place.

In a few moments Eliza Cartwright came out the front door. She let it slam hard, then walked along the bare porch. On her left hip rode a two-year-old boy with a dirty face and a head of curly blond hair. "Whatcha want?" she said as she leaned against a porch post and gave Robbie a hint of a smile.

"How 'bout another kiss?" he said boldly as he handed the reins of his horse to Gil and swaggered closer. The two boys in the tree giggled.

Eliza turned her head slightly to the side and squinted her gray eyes. "I never kissed you," she said as she clinched her lips into a stubborn line. She glanced at Gil.

Gil felt she was playing with them—both of them, like a cat with a caught mouse. He said nothing but looked down at the hard dirt and fumbled with the horses' reins in his hands. Suddenly he realized that Robbie, who had stopped moving toward the porch, must really feel foolish.

"How 'bout last Friday, when you were pickin' apples?"

She rolled her eyes and turned from Robbie to Gil with a can-you-believe-this? look on her face.

"Well, it wasn't a hummingbird," protested Robbie.

"Oh, that little peck on my cheek. I'd almost forgotten."

Standing up straighter, Robbie said bravely, "How 'bout you and me goin' for a walk down by the creek?"

"Can't today," said Eliza as she started toward the door. "Mama's seeing to baby Sarah, so I've gotta take care of Valentine"—she nodded at her little brother and swung him onto to her other hip—"and do *all* the other chores, too." She opened the door, but just before she went inside, she looked back at Robbie and said, "But why don't you come back next Sunday afternoon?" And then she was gone.

More giggles came from the tree above Gil's head.

"There, you see?" said Robbie as he turned around with a triumphant look pasted on his face. "She even invited me back!"

Gil forgot about going to the Cartwrights during the rest of the week. All he could think about was figuring out some way to make a trip to the wilderness of Illinois to find Black Hawk. If he could get to the Ohio River, he could travel down it to the Mississippi River and hook up with some trader or trapper going north.

He was thinking about that very idea as he finished his Sunday dinner. Robbie stood up from the table and said, "You comin', Gil?"

"Ah, what? . . . where?"

Robbie nodded his head in a southwesterly direction. "You know—where I was *invited* for Sunday afternoon."

"Oh! Oh yeah, over to the—"

But Robbie cut him off. "Well, are you comin' or not?" Apparently, Robbie didn't want to announce his interest in Eliza Cartwright to the whole Hamilton household.

"You know," said Robbie as they approached the Cartwright farm a couple hours later, "Eliza's got a younger sister who might suit you."

"You mean that little girl who poked her face

around the house last time? Not hardly!"

"No. There's another one, in between. Maria. She reads books all the time."

"Heavens, how many kids do they have?"

"Not that many. Seven, I think."

"Well, I ain't interested in girls," snorted Gil. "They're jerking you around all the time." But even as he said it, he remembered Eliza's glances as he stood under the chestnut tree in front of her house. He had to admit that she sure was pretty.

Peter Cartwright was home when the boys arrived. It was a pleasant afternoon, and he was reading in a chair on the front porch. "Well, well, it's Gil and . . ."

"Robert. He's my cousin," offered Gil, seeing that Mr. Cartwright couldn't remember Robbie's name.

"Yes. Robert. Well, seems I've heard you mentioned around here lately. You're the Hamilton boy, aren't you?"

"Yes, sir." Robbie blushed, and Gil wondered if he was remembering the last time the preacher had addressed him . . . when he'd been sitting on the wrong side of the meeting.

"Well, Gil, how are your plans for visiting Black Hawk coming along? You got any ideas?"

At that moment Eliza and the sister Gil figured must be Maria came out. The younger girl looked to be about twelve.

"Hi, Robbie," said Eliza without being coy.

"Hi," said Robbie. Without saying, "Glad to meet you," or anything else to Peter Cartwright, Robbie turned his attention from the man to his daughters. "Where are you two goin'?"

"We were going for a walk down by the creek. Wanna come?"

"Sure." Robbie looked expectantly at Gil.

Gil glanced at Peter Cartwright. "Nah. You all go ahead. I'll see you later."

When they left, Gil turned to Peter Cartwright, eager to talk about finding Black Hawk. But the preacher had a deep scowl on his face as he watched the three young people walk across the pasture toward the creek. "Does young Hamilton there have any brothers or sisters?"

"No. Aunt Edith and Uncle George only have Robbie."

"Well, that may be fortunate for you." He smiled at Gil. "With such a large plantation, you should stand to inherit a sizable chunk."

"Not likely," said Gil wryly, thinking how often Aunt Edith reminded him that he wasn't to expect anything. "I think they want to keep it all together."

Cartwright's frown returned to his face as he looked again across the pasture in the direction the others had gone. They were almost out of sight. "Hamilton owns a lot of slaves, doesn't he?"

"About sixty. It's one of the largest plantations around."

"And young Hamilton would stand to inherit them all, wouldn't he." It wasn't a real question, but a statement of fact. The preacher rubbed his chin in his characteristic way. "I sure don't like this slave

business. Importing slaves into the United States has been outlawed for fifteen years, but the evil keeps spreadin' from father to son, and then by marriage from one family to another. One thing's sure—I won't have it infecting my family." The veins on his forehead stuck out and he clinched his teeth.

He stood up and yelled, using his powerful voice that could be heard by five hundred people at a time in an outdoor meeting. "Eliza, Maria," he boomed, dragging out the a's at the end of each name. "Come on back here to the house."

He waited a moment, then yelled even louder, "Do you hear me?"

Very faintly came the answering call, "Yes, Papa."

"Now, boy," said Cartwright sitting back down. "I apologize for changin' the subject. What's your idea for findin' Black Hawk?"

Maria came skipping up the path. Lagging far behind was Eliza, followed by Robbie. When Maria got to the house, she disappeared inside, but Eliza sat in the swing while Robbie stood around hanging on the rope. He talked softly so that neither Gil nor Mr. Cartwright could hear.

Gil told the preacher his idea to go down the Ohio and hitch up with some traders headed north, but the man's attention was clearly distracted by his daughter and Robbie. Finally he said, "Sounds like a good plan, if you can make it work." But there was no heart in his encouragement.

Soon he excused himself and went into the house. Gil felt awkward, not being invited to join Robbie and Eliza, but not knowing what else to do.

A short while later, Cartwright came out again to tell Eliza that it was time for supper. He did not invite Gil and Robbie to stay. In fact, he said nothing to Robbie, and without looking Gil in the eye said, "I'll be prayin' the Lord meets your needs, son."

As Gil and his cousin rode away from the house, Robbie snorted, "I must say, old man Cartwright's none too hospitable—didn't even invite us to supper. How'd you stand takin' that trip with him?"

But they had just turned from the Cartwright lane east onto the road from Hopkinsville toward home when Cartwright came galloping up behind them. "Hamilton!" he called to Robbie as his horse jarred to a stop, "I hope you don't take personal offense at this, but you're not welcome to call on my daughter again."

Quick with his tongue, Robbie said, "How's that, Reverend? You still hold that camp meetin' incident against me?"

"Nope," said the preacher, trying to calm his excited, prancing horse. "But as you know, I'm against slavery . . . and I don't want my daughter getting involved with someone from a slave-owning family. That's all."

"Oh!" Robbie huffed. "So, I'm not good enough for you?"

"I didn't say that. I hardly know you. But if you started courtin' her, it might lead to . . . to something more, and I don't want any of my children to inherit slaves. That'd make them slavers, too."

To Gil's embarrassment, Robbie laughed right out loud. Gil figured his cousin must be terribly angry to be so rude to an older man—and a preacher, at that! "Well, now," said Robbie, "since nearly everyone in these parts owns slaves, and since you have so many daughters, Mr. Cartwright, just how are you gonna stop at least some of them from gettin' mixed up with the likes of us? You gonna lock 'em up in a woodshed until they're old maids?"

Chapter 8

The Wilderness Hope

PETER CARTWRIGHT'S HORSE twisted and turned under him while the preacher stared with fiery black eyes at Robbie. Suddenly he spurred his horse and galloped back down his lane without attempting to answer Robbie's question.

"He thinks he's so almighty better than the rest of us!" Robbie spat. "But I still want to know how he's gonna keep his daughters from marryin' into a slaveholdin' family."

Gil shrugged. All this talk about marrying! Why, Robbie was only fourteen. Still . . . an interesting thought crossed Gil's mind. *He* wasn't a slaveholder and wouldn't inherit any of the Hamilton slaves. Maybe Peter Cartwright wouldn't mind if he married one of the Cartwright girls—well, someday.

But Gil learned Cartwright's solution to the problem a week later through local gossip. "I hear that travelin' preacher's leavin' the state," Aunt Edith said to her husband as the family sat on the veranda to enjoy the cool evening breezes. Gil and Robbie were playing checkers while Uncle George smoked his pipe and Aunt Edith knitted.

Gil looked up, startled, but his uncle continued to stare toward the hazy, blue horizon.

"I expect you'll be glad to see him go after what he did to you over at the Pritchards' last month," prodded Aunt Edith, intent on getting a response from her husband.

Finally, Uncle George said, "I couldn't care less one way or the other." And he went on puffing on his pipe. After a minute he completely changed the subject. "I have been thinking about clearing off that parcel of ours down near the river. It could make a nice tobacco field, don't you think?"

Realizing that the conversation was passing on from the mention of Peter Cartwright, Gil asked, "Where's Reverend Cartwright goin'?"

"From what I hear, they're headed for Illinois," replied Aunt Edith. "But why anyone would move to that Godforsaken wilderness, I'll never know."

"That's obvious," Robbie said knowingly as he took one of Gil's kings. "Illinois is a free state. Mr. High-and-Mighty Cartwright is getting his kids away from all us slave-owning sinners." He laughed to himself. "I guess I chased him clean out of the territory."

"You what?" said Uncle George, pulling his pipe out of his mouth and looking at his son.

Cautiously Robbie told the story, uncertain what his parents would think of him flirting with Eliza Cartwright.

"My word! You should be ashamed of yourself," scolded his mother. "At your age—"

"Now hold on, Edith," interrupted Uncle George. "That preacher chased Robbie out of his meetin'. I think it's only fittin' that Robbie chase him out of Kentucky." And he roared with laughter, something he rarely did.

Gil was only listening with half an ear. An idea was forming in his mind. "When are they leaving?" he asked casually.

"Well," said Aunt Edith, "Mary Pritchard's all broken up over it, of course. She said Cartwright's leavin' right away to survey the territory, but who knows when they'll actually be moving?"

Gil rode over to the Cartwrights' early the next morning hoping that the preacher had not yet left.

Gil found Cartwright in his small barn replacing a strap on a packsaddle for his supply horse. "I heard you were headin' for Illinois," he said, coming right to the point. "Could I ride with you? It might be my best chance to find Black Hawk." *And my mother,* he thought.

"Hmm," said Cartwright. "Your interest in Illinois had slipped my mind, but . . . this ain't no leisure trip, son. Fall's comin'; it's late to be travelin' at all. We wouldn't have time to take side trips lookin' for Indians."

"That's all right," said Gil. "If I could just get to that part of the country, I might be able to learn something. Please take me, Reverend Cartwright. Please!"

"Well, my brother-in-law Robert Gaines, and an old preacher friend of mine, Charles Holliday, should be here soon. They're goin' with me, and we were hoping to leave in a day or so." Cartwright stopped working on the saddle strap and rubbed his chin. "Of course, you'd have to get permission from your aunt and uncle."

"I'll go ask them right now . . . if you'll take me, that is."

"Well, let's go see what they say," Cartwright said with a wave of his hand.

Gil hadn't expected Cartwright to come, too—it was a long ride—but in the end it was a good thing. At first Uncle George and Aunt Edith thought it was a crazy idea. But then the whole story came out about Gil finding out from Andrew Jackson that Black Hawk, the Indian who took his mother, was from the Sauk tribe located in Illinois. Gil was determined to get there . . . somehow. He wanted to know if his mother was still alive.

Whether from compassion or frustration—Gil wasn't sure which—Aunt Edith turned to her husband and said, "The boy can't let it go, George. Goodness knows how many times he talks about her. Maybe it's best he find out the truth."

Gil knew Uncle George lost no love on Peter Cartwright, so he was surprised when his uncle suddenly changed his mind.

"That's wild country," his uncle said gruffly. "I don't want the boy roaming through it alone. Will you promise to keep him with you?"

"You have my word," Peter Cartwright agreed.

Two days later young Gilbert Hamilton was with Peter Cartwright, Cartwright's brother-in-law Robert Gaines, and the elderly Reverend Charles Holliday as the small party rode through Hopkinsville and headed northwest to explore the Illinois wilderness.

Northern Illinois was only sparsely populated by white people, but since Black Hawk's tribe was located in that area, the travelers agreed to Gil's requests to swing through that wilderness to learn what they could about any white women living among the Sauks. The plan also fit Peter Cartwright's goals because he wanted to discover where the most distant white people had settled. "That'll show me where we need to set up new circuits."

Circuit-riding preachers ministered in remote

areas where too few people lived to support a local church. A preacher like Cartwright set up a route that he traveled once a month visiting families in their homes, sometimes gathering two or three neighboring families together for a preaching service. In this way each preacher ministered to a "congregation" of three to four hundred people once a month—

a larger church than they would get by any other means. Every year the “members” of a circuit traveled to a central place for a camp meeting.

Most people welcomed circuit-riding preachers not only for the chance to worship and receive Christian instruction but because the preachers provided a primary source of news, delivered mail, and sometimes brought medicine and other emergency supplies.

The late August air hung heavy and hot day after day as the Cartwright company traveled up the Wabash River valley, then cut north until they hit the Kankakee River. They followed it northwest downstream until it joined the Illinois River flowing west. This was country only thinly settled by white people.

“These people need the gospel, but there aren't enough of them yet to make a circuit,” Cartwright decided as they detoured around a large swampy area created by the Illinois River flooding its banks. “We'll stop at Fort Clark, but after that, we'd better head south to find more people.”

“What about the Indian villages we've passed?” Gil asked. “Wouldn't they make a good circuit?”

“They don't stay in those villages year around,” Cartwright informed him. “These Indians are nomadic. They regularly go on hunting trips or wage wars or attend big ceremonial feasts with other tribes. It suits them better for us to build a mission they can come to instead of chasin' them all over tarnation.”

They had followed the Illinois River west toward the Mississippi when it suddenly turned south—away from the area where Andrew Jackson said Black Hawk lived. At first Gil hoped it was only a temporary diversion, but by the time they arrived at Fort Clark the next afternoon they had traveled thirty miles south, and he was beginning to worry.

At the fort, Gil was determined to find out some information about Black Hawk. The first person he spoke to was a young soldier who had been there only a month, but he sent Gil to the trading post to talk to the old man who ran it.

"Yeah, I know Black Hawk," said the old-timer from behind the counter. Being nearly bald, he looked as if his hair had slid off his head and collected on his face in his huge beard. The yellowed beard was so thick that it hid his mouth completely; the only way Gil could tell the old trader was speaking was by the way his beard bobbled up and down with his words. "We're pretty good friends, actually. His village is about fifty miles northwest of here as the crow flies, right where the Rock River dumps into the Mississippi."

"Have you ever heard of a white woman living with them?"

"Nah, there ain't no white women at Saukenuk." The old man stabbed a stick of jerky through his beard and bit off a piece. "However," he said as he chewed, "come to think of it . . . there is one blue-eyed squaw in the village, but she ain't white. Who you lookin' for?"

Gil swallowed. "My mother. She was taken by

Black Hawk in the War of 1812. She had blue eyes. Do you . . . do you think that blue-eyed squaw could be her?"

The man frowned. "This squaw's as Indian as they come, son. She probably inherited those blue eyes from some trapper or maybe even a Spaniard a century ago. Who knows? But I can tell you one thing, I never heard her speak any English."

Gil left the trading post bewildered. One minute the old man was saying there weren't any white women at Saukenuk . . . the next he was talking about a woman with blue eyes, just like his mama. But then the old-timer seemed certain she was Indian. What was the truth?

The only thing I can do is discover the truth for myself, he thought.

But Peter Cartwright had also made a discovery. "I'm sorry, Gil, but there's no way we can make a trip up there right now. I just learned that a vote's set to be held to determine whether the whole State of Illinois will be free or slave. So we're goin' south to do a little preachin'."

"But—you can't leave yet!" Gil protested. "We're so close to finding my mother. It would only take a few days."

"I can't risk it, Gil. If I'm going to move my family here, this state had better remain free. I've got to get down among the organized counties—where most white folks have settled—and speak to people, see what their mood is. Maybe later you can come back this way to look for your mother."

"But there're people up this way who need converting, aren't there?"

"So there are . . . but as you've seen, not many of 'em. Everyone's soul is important, but slavery is a votin' matter where numbers count. It will be to everyone's betterment if this state remains free. I must go south. Sorry, Gil."

Gil was feeling desperate. "Then let me go on up to Rock River myself. I can make it, and when I find her, we'll catch up and join you."

After a long moment, Cartwright shook his head slowly. "You know, Gil, if it were up to me, I'd let you go. I reckon you could make it on your own, but I promised your aunt and uncle that I'd keep you with me, and I'm a man of my word. You'll have to come south with us."

Realizing it was hopeless to argue further, Gil's shoulders slumped and he turned away. He slipped into a blue mood, moving like he was in a dream as the travelers left the fort that very afternoon.

Cartwright's party traveled down the western bank of the Illinois River and camped in the open that night. The next day they pushed on hard until they came to a small, solitary cabin overlooking the river.

The man who came to the door was a wiry old man with no teeth, but he was friendly and invited the travelers to spend the night. As he served up beans and cornbread for supper, the man announced, "This here's gonna be a town some day. You mark my word."

"How can you know such a thing as that?" asked Charles Holliday, the old preacher traveling with them.

"Because I'm gonna build it, that's why!" the man grinned, revealing his toothless gums. "Half a mile yonder the Sangamon River flows east, straight to Springfield. Why, this here's the best place to cross the Illinois River if you want to travel up the Sangamon to Springfield. Even now there's some boat traffic on its way to St. Louis from Springfield. Anytime you got a natural intersection like that, it's a good place for a town."

Taking the old man's advice about a good fording place, the next day the travelers crossed the Illinois and rode east along the Sangamon River. By afternoon they were seeing more and more signs of civilization. Their route grew from a faint game trail to a double path that had been cut by occasional wagons. And then they came upon scattered cabins of homesteaders.

"So this is Springfield," Peter Cartwright said wryly as they finally rode into a dingy little town. "Ain't much to it, is there? But since it is an up-and-coming frontier town, guess this is the place we need to do our preachin'."

Springfield consisted of a few smoky, hastily built cabins and two little buildings that called themselves stores. Except for a couple of plows and kegs of nails, Gil decided they could have carried off the entire inventory on their backs.

For three weeks Peter Cartwright, Robert Gaines,

and Charles Holliday preached almost nonstop to the townspeople and those in the surrounding homesteads. Winter was approaching, and they'd soon have to return to Kentucky. The only time Cartwright took off from visiting people and preaching against slavery was to buy a six-hundred-acre farm with a two-room cabin on it. This he rented out so there would be some crops to harvest the next fall when he and his family moved to Illinois.

Sitting around waiting for Peter Cartwright to finish preaching was hard on Gil. Restless and bored, he found some work helping a man build a new brick inn not more than a mile from Cartwright's new farm, which earned him a few dollars. But it didn't do much to lift his spirit.

His thoughts turned bitter. After wondering about his mother for so many years . . . after riding all the way from Kentucky . . . he'd come within a couple days of finding her! The old man had *said* there was a blue-eyed squaw. But tomorrow they were heading back for Kentucky . . . and finding his mother seemed more impossible than ever.

Chapter 9

When Lightning Strikes Twice

THAT WINTER AND SPRING were miserable for Gil. After returning home to the Hamilton plantation, all he could think of was having missed his mother. He was so gloomy his aunt claimed his mood affected everyone and everything around him.

But it wasn't until she said, "I can't wait 'til you're out on your own, Gilbert," that he decided that was exactly what he needed to do—set out on his own. There was no future for him on the Hamilton plantation. Even though he was only fourteen, he wouldn't be the first boy to strike out on his own at such a young age.

And Gil had an idea. Peter Cartwright was moving to a six-hundred-acre farm in Illinois—but he was off preaching most of the year. *He can't even keep up with his little farm here in Kentucky,* thought Gil. *He'll certainly need some help building up such a large new place.* So Gil suggested to Cartwright that he become the family's hired hand. "One way or another, I aim to go to Illinois and find my mother," declared Gil. "If you could provide me with a situation, that would be a big start."

"It's a 'situation' you want, is it? Well, I suppose I could use some help with the move and getting settled—but I couldn't pay much and even that might not last long."

"All I need is a start," said Gil. "If the work plays out, I can pick up something else later."

"We couldn't give you a place to live, either," said Peter, rubbing his chin. "We got us nothin' more than a two-room cabin for seven kids and the missus and me. You'd have to find that for yourself."

"Maybe I could find something in Springfield or . . . how about that new brick inn in Claysville? You know, the one I worked on. It's not more than a mile east of your homestead."

After thinking about it for a few moments, Cartwright finally said, "I'll take you on one condition. I know your main objective is to find your mother. I sympathize and want to help you out whenever I can. However, if I hire you to work for us, then that's your *first* obligation as long as I need you. When I can give you time off to look for your mother,

I will, but I don't want you runnin' off when I need you most. Is that understood?"

"Yes sir," said Gil with a big smile. "I'm your man!"

During the months that followed, Gil spent all his free time getting ready to leave Kentucky. In a slave society it wasn't easy to find work for pay. The small jobs a kid might do to earn a little cash were done by slaves.

Strangely enough, the thing that provided him a little money to outfit himself was the use of Robbie's hounds. Fifteen-year-old Robbie had started spending all his time playing cards and gambling with his friends. He seldom ran the dogs but was glad for Gil to take them out whenever he wished.

Gil was able to catch several foxes and raccoons and sell their skins. The raccoons weren't worth much, but the fox pelts earned him the few dollars he needed.

The big day was October 23, 1824. After a civil goodbye to the Hamiltons, Gil rode the fifteen miles to the Cartwright farm, equipped with his horse, a secondhand rifle, a new rain slicker, a bedroll, and a heavy winter coat. ("You better get something warm," Cartwright had advised one day. "I hear those prairie blizzards make the winters around here seem like a summer squall.")

As they set out, Gil drove the overloaded

Cartwright wagon with Cartwright's wife, Frances, on the wagon seat and Eliza and the youngest children in back. Peter Cartwright rode ahead to check out the road. Twelve-year-old Maria and nine-year-old Cynthia herded the stock along behind.

Gil felt uneasy about Eliza riding on the wagon so close to him. It was okay for Mrs. Cartwright and the youngest children to ride, but why couldn't Eliza walk? She sat on an old trunk facing backwards, sniffling into an old rag she was using for a handkerchief. Her eyes and nose were red and swollen, and she hadn't said a word since Gil had arrived at the house that morning. *She's crying about leaving home,* thought Gil. *Maybe she misses Robbie. Huh! That must be it. She really must've liked him after all and is angry about moving.*

It was hard work hanging on to the reins as the draft horses pulled the heavy wagon, creaking and groaning, over the rugged road. Keeping out of deep ruts that caused the wagon to tip precariously took Gil's constant attention.

By noon the sky had clouded over, and a light drizzle made Gil's work more difficult as the trail became slick.

"Eliza," Mrs. Cartwright urged, "wrap up in that wool blanket and put this oilcloth over you. That cold is too bad to take any chances of it getting worse."

"Yes, Mama," said Eliza, and then she sneezed.

Feeling foolish, Gil realized there might be a valid reason why Eliza was riding rather than walking. Her sniffles might be from a cold rather than from grief over leaving Robbie. For just a moment, Gil looked back with new interest at the girl huddled among the furniture and household belongings—but it was a moment too long. Just then, the left front wagon wheel caught on a huge root and caused the wagon to lurch dangerously. After that, he tried harder to keep his attention on his driving.

That evening when the rain ended, the clouds lifted in the west to reveal a blazing sunset. The damp countryside smelled like freshly cut hay, and hope filled the future for everyone in the Cartwright party as they made camp by a small brook with a large, open meadow before them. They had traveled fourteen miles, not far over established roads but far enough for their first day out.

Eliza still carried a handkerchief that she frequently applied to her red nose, but she seemed much better and chipped right in gathering wood and helping to put up the family tent.

Once he had picketed the horses and cows downstream from the camp, Gil arranged his bedroll under the wagon to keep off any dew or in case there was more rain.

Supper was simple—bread baked before they left, a hard-boiled egg each, and all the apples they could eat from a nearby tree. "Do you think Johnny Appleseed planted that tree?" Eliza asked her father as her teeth snapped into the tart, red fruit.

"I expect so," grinned Peter. "He's been all through this Ohio River Valley plantin' his trees. Now they say he's moved west. Maybe we'll find some of his trees in Illinois. What do you think, children?"

"Are there any on our new farm?" asked Cartwright's son Madison.

"Don't know," said Peter. "Guess you'll have to explore."

The next four days passed uneventfully except that the travelers never went as many miles per day as they hoped. Eliza's cold improved considerably, and late one afternoon she was sitting beside Gil on the driver's seat as they were coming out of some rolling hills. "Don't you think this is the most boring country you've ever seen?" she said.

"What do you mean?"

"Well, there aren't any mountains to tell your directions from, just these little hills. Will it be like this on the prairie?"

"Take a look," said Gil as they came over a rise. Out in front of them stretched the beginnings of the great prairie. The grassy plain stretched unbroken except for scattered groves of trees toward the horizon. At a distance of a mile or two out onto the prairie sat two cabins with thin trails of smoke rising lazily from them—homes for other settlers.

"Ugh," said Eliza, "why didn't Papa tell me it was going to be so flat? I never would have come."

Gil pulled hard on the reins to restrain the horses in their steep descent to the valley floor some two hundred feet below the hill's crest. He looked out at the panorama before them. "What's the matter with prairie?" he asked. "A person can see forever. I think it's magnificent!"

"I suppose *you* would!" she said sarcastically.

The rutted road dove down the hill, tilting the wagon sharply forward. Gil braced himself and gripped the reins as he glanced sideways at Eliza. What did she mean? Her nose was wrinkled up like she'd caught a whiff of sour milk, and the mockery in her comment stabbed him . . . and angered him, too. But why should he care what she thought?

Suddenly, the wagon lurched to one side as the left front wheel dropped into a small wash partially hidden by grass. The wagon tipped farther, and Mrs. Cartwright jumped off and rolled on the ground with baby Sarah in her arms. Gil grabbed for the brake, but it did no good. With a slow, creaking grind the straining vehicle tipped all the way over onto its side.

The children screamed as the wagon smashed to the ground sending pots and pans clashing and chickens in their willow cages squawking. Out of the corner of his eye, Gil saw Madison and Wealthy—the two middle boys—fly over his head and land clear. Then he heard Valentine scream, "Mommy!"

In spite of Gil's last-ditch efforts, the horses spooked and tried to bolt down the hill. Their lunging in their harnesses caused the wagon to continue its roll. At the last second, Gil leaped out of the way before the contraption made another quarter turn and smashed completely upside down in a great pile of clattering junk.

“Whoa! Whoa!” urged Gil. Finally, the frantic beasts calmed down, and Gil turned to look back at the damage. All four wagon wheels turned slowly above the cloud of dust. The wagon looked like a pig on its back with its feet in the air.

"Mommy! Mommy!" wailed little Valentine as he toddled around the back of the wreck. To see him safe and sound made his cries the sweetest sound Gil had ever heard.

Peter Cartwright came galloping up the hill. "What happened? Is everyone all right?" he yelled, glaring at Gil.

"I think so," said his wife, picking herself up from the ground where she and baby Sarah had fallen. Maria and Cynthia were hurrying the livestock over the crest of the hill, and everyone soon gathered around the overturned wagon, surveying the damage.

"What's that?" said Mrs. Cartwright, startled.

"What?" said Cynthia.

"That cry! I heard someone crying. Someone's under there. Who's missing?"

"Where's Eliza?" yelled Peter as he scrambled around trying to look under the wagon. "Eliza? Is that you under there? Are you all right?"

"Ye-es . . . I think so," came the muffled voice. "Just get me outta here."

Gil, still trying to hold the horses, edged closer to see and help.

"Eliza's trapped!" Peter barked. "Help me lift this so we can get her out." But when everyone—even the smaller children—stepped up to lend a hand, he said, "No, no. You children stay back. This thing could slip and crush you. Maria, you hold the horses so this reckless lummox can help," he said, glaring at Gil.

There was much fumbling and grunting as Peter, his wife, and Gil tried to lift the edge of the wagon, but it wouldn't budge. Eliza remained trapped.

It seemed to Gil that the only way to get the wagon off Eliza was to use the horses to pull it off, but he felt so guilty for having caused the accident that he didn't want to say anything more. But when even a pole used as a lever failed to lift the wagon's side, he spoke up. "What if we attach the harness traces from the horses to the downhill side of the wagon and use them to roll it over until it's off her?"

"What? Are you crazy?" snapped Peter. "You want the thing to roll all the way to the bottom of the hill? That's everything we own!"

"No," said Gil, thinking fast. "We could attach a rope between that tree up the hill and the other side of the wagon. Then we could let it out a little at a time to stop the rolling when the wagon is righted."

Peter Cartwright was skeptical, but the more he considered the suggestion, the more it seemed like the only way.

As soon as the horses started the wagon on another roll down hill, Eliza scrambled out from under it. Gil urged the horses on a few more steps while Peter let out the safety line from above. When the rickety wagon crashed again onto its wheels—still tipping at an awful slant—Peter tied off the line. "Whoa, there! Easy now!" Gil cried to the horses, which were still spooked from the earlier accident.

Though Eliza was terrified, dirty, and bruised, she seemed otherwise uninjured. Frances Cartwright hugged her oldest daughter, wiped the dirt from her face, and hugged her some more. Even though everyone was all right, both adults and children felt shaken.

It was nearly dark by the time they reloaded the wagon. Ahead of them was the rest of the challenging, downhill slope. They decided not to attempt descending it in the dark.

They retraced their steps a short distance up the hill to level ground and set up camp under an old tree. "We're all so tired," said Mrs. Cartwright. "Let's not put up the tent; the weather's clear." Wearily, Peter built a fire near the tree, and they all spread their blankets on the ground and fell asleep.

Some time in the middle of the night, Gil roused himself to find a more comfortable position and noticed that a breeze had come up. The flames of the fire had gone out, but the wind made the coals glow comfortingly. He snuggled into his bedroll and went back to sleep.

A loud cracking sound, then a horrible yell ripped Gil from his sleep. He whipped his blanket off. A few yards away, in the light of early dawn, he could see a man standing with legs apart and arms wrapped around the fallen trunk of the old tree that had spread its scraggly limbs above their camp. Splinters of a jagged stump stabbed their silhouette into the sky. For an instant Gil thought he was dreaming of a giant who had broken off the tree, but then he realized it was Peter Cartwright. Somehow the tree had fallen—and was lying directly across nine-year-old Cynthia!

The tree was obviously too heavy for Cartwright to be holding it up; it was simply resting where it had fallen. "Don't just sit there staring, boy! Run for help!" grunted Cartwright desperately, trying to lift some of the weight off the girl.

Gil jumped up, pulled on his boots, and snapped his suspenders over his shoulders. Without a coat or hat, he tore down the mountain toward the two cabins he had seen the evening before.

Twenty minutes later Gil stumbled up to the first cabin, just as a man came out of the door. He had a bucket in his hand and looked like he was setting out to do the morning chores.

"Help!" wheezed Gil, spilling out the tale of the tragedy.

But the man just squinted his eyes at Gil. "Likely story," he snorted. "Could be you're a fox tryin' to call me off my nest so you can steal my eggs."

"W-what?"

"Never mind. Thieves always comin' through with a sob story—"

"No, no! You got it all wrong! There's been a terrible accident. A tree fell on us during the night—"

"Ha! You said this . . . this accident happened this mornin'. Now you're saying 'twas last night. Caught ya! You're not being straight with me. Oh, yeah. We get lots of crazy people comin' through here. No way I'm goin' off and leavin' my family unguarded."

Gil looked desperately toward the other cabin.

"Forget it. That's my mother's place. She ain't got nothin' for you. Now get outta here before I fill your britches full of buckshot." And the man reached for a gun that was leaning next to the cabin door.

Gil turned away in despair and headed back toward the hill. The sun had just come up when he finally got back to their camp . . . and he could tell by the silent, stricken faces of the family that little Cynthia was dead.

Stunned, he set to work helping Peter saw the log off the child's dead body. Little was said until Peter mumbled, "Who says lightning doesn't strike twice in the same spot?"

Suddenly a dam of emotions seemed to break loose, and everyone began crying and wailing. Frances and the children begged to return to civilization in Kentucky. Even Peter was tempted. "A country where people won't even come to a man's aid when tragedy strikes is too much—just too much," he said angrily. "It ain't human. Maybe we should go back. Maybe I made a big mistake."

Peter wiped his sleeve across his forehead. "Maybe God didn't lead me out here," he groaned, more to himself than anyone else. "These accidents don't seem natural . . . maybe they're a warning."

Chapter 10

Under the Cat's Paw

GIL STARTED TO WORRY. Was this to be the end of his move to Illinois? Was Peter Cartwright going to turn back to Kentucky just when they were on the frontier of a new land?

"You can't turn back now," pleaded Gil.

"Why not?" said Peter, looking out over the prairie to the cabins of the man who wouldn't help them. "If those are the kind of people who live out here . . ." His voice trailed off.

"But isn't that why you preach the gospel?" asked Gil. "To change people like that?"

Cartwright looked sharply at Gil. "What do you know? You

haven't even become a Christian yet."

The words stung. In spite of how strongly Cartwright preached, the evangelist had never pressured Gil. He merely preached the gospel, apparently confident that the message would persuade Gil when the time was right, but now he seemed scornful. What was happening?

The cause of the tree's falling became obvious as they worked to clear it from Cynthia's little body. The tree was full of dry rot except for an inch of sound wood right under the bark. The fire had weakened what remained of the trunk enough for a slight wind to topple it.

No one spoke as the realization sunk in. These weren't freak accidents or warnings. The first one had been caused by Gil's distraction; the second because Peter Cartwright had made a mistake by building a fire at the base of a dead tree.

A map of grief and resignation etched itself in Cartwright's craggy face as he carefully wrapped his daughter's body in a blanket and laid her in the feed trough strapped to the side of the wagon. All the while, Mrs. Cartwright and the other children cried softly and held one another in a little huddle. Gil stood back not knowing quite what to do.

Then the preacher got on his horse and simply said, "Time we get movin'."

When everyone was in place on the wagon or herding the animals, Peter Cartwright headed down the hill to the prairie. The children's sobbing grew louder as they saw which way he was going, but no one argued with him.

Seeing their pain, Gil did not dare smile with joy for getting his wish to continue on to Illinois.

As they rode past the farm of the heartless settler, the man stopped working in his garden and leaned on his hoe while he watched them slowly pass. He didn't wave or offer any greeting.

They traveled in silence until nearly noon when Peter swung his horse in beside the wagon and said to Frances, "There are some Christian people who live in Hamilton County. If we can make it there by tonight, we'll bury Cynthia with them."

"Does that mean we're in Illinois now?"

"Ever since we crossed the river yesterday."

They were in Illinois! Gil hadn't even known it! A thrill went through him, but he said nothing.

After burying Cynthia, traveling over the open prairie seemed to Gil like sailing on an open sea. The small groves of trees at which they stopped for meals and to make camp were like islands—the only sources of firewood and fresh water.

The Cartwrights finally arrived at their new home in Sangamon county on November 15. The weather was mild, and Gil wanted to leave immediately for a trip north to look for his mother.

"Now wait a minute," Cartwright reminded him. "I brought you out here on the condition that you would work for me, didn't I?"

"Yes, sir . . . and I *have* been workin' for you." He hesitated to say he had done a good job, considering the accident.

"Well, I still need you. There're squash, pumpkins, potatoes, and corn in the fields. We need to harvest those in order to survive the winter. Those renters who lived here put a little hay in the barn, but there isn't enough hay or wood to last the winter. When I give you time off, then you can take your trip."

Gil knew that was only fair, but it just felt like he was wasting more time before he could find his mother.

"Just be patient," said Peter. "In the spring, as soon as it's safe to travel, there should be time for a trip before the fields are ready to work. I'll even go with you . . . at least part way," he offered. "I need to develop this Sangamon Circuit."

But Gil did not want to wait. Each day he worked hard hoping that bad weather would hold off long enough for him make one quick trip north.

Then in mid-December, Cartwright announced, "Well, Gil, I think we about did it. Why don't you take a little time off for the holidays. You got enough money to hold you, don't you?"

"Yes, Mr. Cartwright. I appreciate what you've been payin' me, sir."

"Well, if you can get some work over at Claysville where you're staying, feel free to take it until I need you next spring . . . or until we take that trip up north," he added with a broad grin.

Gil had no intention of waiting till spring. A couple light snows had fallen but most had blown away, and the creeks and marshes had frozen solid. It looked to Gil like good traveling conditions. He raced back to his rooming house, gathered his gear, and was on his way that very afternoon.

He rode west along the south bank of the Sangamon to the Illinois River, retracing the route he had traveled with Peter more than a year before. Where the two rivers joined, he could see the homestead of the old man they had stayed with before. It looked like two more cabins had been built. He called and called, hoping the man had a boat and could help him cross.

Finally the old man came out. "Can't help you!" he yelled back. He motioned downstream. "You can cross 'bout twenty yards down by them bushes!"

The crossing was treacherous. Leading his horse, Gil waded in swiftly moving water halfway up his thighs, feeling his way along with a stick to avoid rocks and holes. By the time he staggered out on the other side, his feet were so numb from the cold that he couldn't even feel his toes.

He stayed with the toothless old man that night. "I ought to charge you. How else am I ever gonna make any money? . . . but you're young. Say, where you headed this time of the year?"

"Saukenuk."

The man shook his head. "Not good! Winter can hit with a fury out here. And if you don't respect it, you can die."

Gil thanked the man for his hospitality—and advice—but he was too eager to turn back now.

Two days later, as Gil traveled north, he had the strange feeling that someone was watching him. He guided his horse along the narrow strip of land between the river's west bank and the sandstone bluffs that rose above it. They sheltered him from the bite of the winter wind. He glanced behind him but saw nothing unusual in the bare woods of the river bottom. Above, the low clouds had that dull, white, thick look that often meant snow, and Gil wondered whether he should have heeded the old man's advice.

I'm just anxious about the weather, Gil told himself as he glanced behind again. *No one would be following me out here.* But he couldn't shake his suspicions.

Then, when he had almost succeeded in putting the notion out of his mind, he caught a glimpse of something moving along the rim of the sandstone bluff not far behind him. His heart lurched, and then relaxed as he figured out what he'd seen: a patch of tawny fur, white at the bottom fading to almost black near the top. *Just a deer.* He smiled.

He took a deep breath of relief as he rode on. But the more he thought about what he'd seen—just a small patch of fur moving between a tree and a rock—he began to feel uncomfortable again. It hadn't moved like a deer. In that split second, it had swung down and up and then out of sight, a movement more fluid and smooth than any deer he'd ever seen.

He looked back over his shoulder at the rocky rim. There was nothing there. Touching his heels to his horse's flank, he rode on, driving his horse through wild rose brambles. The thicket was so dense that he forgot his fears as he picked his way forward.

Just as he reached another wooded area where the ground was relatively free from underbrush, scattered snowflakes drifted down from above.

Suddenly, stones clattered down the bluff.

Something was up there! And a deer wouldn't follow a person just out of curiosity.

Gil scanned the rim, riding faster until he came to a cut in the rocks where a stream bounced its way down from the tableland above to join the river. Then, just as his horse crossed the creek, a great cat leaped from the lip of the south wall of the narrow gorge to the north wall. It was pursuing Gil.

A cougar. It has to be a cougar! Gil remembered seeing the skin of one of the huge cats tacked to a barn door back in Kentucky. It had been six feet long, not counting the tail.

Dense woods prevented Gil from increasing his speed. He watched the top of the bluff more closely and caught another glimpse of the great cat as it peered over the rim at him. There was no question; it was hunting him.

But why? Why is a lion stalking me? I'm a man on horseback. He could think of no answer, but stranger things had happened. He had to keep calm.

At that point the bluffs were closer to the river's edge, and Gil had to slow down because slippery boulders and tangles of dead trees piled up by spring floods hindered his progress.

Finally he broke into a small, open area where the bluff curved away from the river for a short distance, and he galloped across the small meadow. Snow was falling faster, but in the open space he decided what to do—he would go on the offensive. If the cat kept coming, Gil would be the hunter, not the hunted. He drew his rifle, cocked it, and checked the priming before he got to the other side of the tiny meadow where the cliffs and the river nearly met again.

There were several feet of ice along the edge of the river's dark water, but by picking his way along a narrow path between the ice and the bluff, Gil made it around the point. He found what he needed. Huge rocks had fallen from the bluff creating stairsteps to the rim above. He grounded his horse below the overhanging bluff and climbed.

A scream pierced the woods and echoed between the rocky walls of the river valley. It sounded like a terrified woman in pain. Had the cat attacked someone else? Gil froze.

Down below, his horse snorted and sidestepped, its ears flat against its head, the whites of its eyes showing as it reared its head.

Gil doubted anyone else was in the woods. The scream must have come from the cat. He remembered people saying there was nothing more frightening than a cougar's scream. Now he knew why.

He continued climbing. If the lion persisted in following him, he wanted to be up on the top in time to shoot it before it caught up to him. The cat would not expect him to meet it on its own ground. It would be watching below. Surprise would be Gil's edge.

He pulled himself over the lip of the rocks, and there, not forty feet away, came the cat bounding right toward him. Somehow he swung his rifle around and pulled the trigger. He was half kneeling and the recoil of the deafening blast nearly knocked him back over the edge. But at the last second the cat saw him, swerved to the side, and catapulted out into space over the edge of the bluff.

Whether by accident or intention, the cougar landed on the back of Gil's horse. The screams and cries of both animals were terrible as Gil scrambled to his feet and tried to reload his rifle. But by the time he succeeded and stumbled to the brink of the bluff, the cat had run off and his horse had bolted across the narrow strip of ice and into the river. The water was deep and swift, and Gil watched in horror as his horse floated downstream, swimming hard for the opposite side. He whistled and called, but in a few minutes his horse was out of sight in the swirling snow and black water.

Gil climbed down the bluff and hurried south, hoping to catch a glimpse of his horse on the other side. The storm worsened, and night came without him having seen a sign of his animal. He camped in a small cave but slept only fitfully as he tried to keep a fire going with the flint and steel he carried. He didn't want to take any chances on the cat returning. Once he heard it scream again, but it sounded far away. Had it swum the river and attacked his horse?

Morning came and Gil's stomach growled with hunger. There was nothing he could do about it. The raging storm kept him a prisoner in the tiny cave for two days. When the wind finally dropped, Gil struggled back the way he'd come through waist-deep drifts, watching the far bank of the river. But there was no sign of his horse.

Being without a horse in the wilderness was bad enough, but the horse had also carried all his provisions in the saddlebags. The old man had warned him that if he didn't respect the winter, it could kill him.

As he trudged south along the river, a knot of fear settled in his empty stomach. He knew he would be lucky, not to find his mother as he had hoped, but just to get home alive.

Chapter 11

Saukenuk

WINTER IN CLAYSVILLE was boring and expensive. Pierre Lamone, the owner of the boardinghouse, was still finishing the interior of some of the rooms, so there was work to do, but when he was away on business, he wouldn't trust Gil with big jobs. "Plane these boards until they're smooth and straight," he would say, "and when I get back from St. Louis in a week or so, I'll show you how I want the doorframe built." His wife allowed Gil to wash dishes, chop wood, and carry out the garbage, but otherwise she wouldn't allow anyone in her kitchen.

The pennies Gil earned from these small jobs did not pay for his room and board, and each week he had to shell out money he'd saved working for Cartwright. He worried about going broke. Even if he did make it through the winter, how was he ever going to replace his horse?

Maybe I ought to pray, he thought. He had prayed hard after the cougar attack. He had prayed to find his horse and as he huddled in the cave and as he'd plowed through the drifts toward home. He prayed, too, when he had fallen through the snow into a swamp. He had cried out to God with tears running down his face. But had God heard?

How could he know? He never found his horse, but he did make it back alive to the old man's cabin at the fork of the rivers . . . though just barely. What did it mean?

The Cartwrights invited him to Sunday dinner each week. That would have been a good place to discuss God, but with Eliza sitting across the table, looking at him with her gray eyes and sometimes smiling, he never seemed to have the courage to bring up the topic. He was embarrassed to talk about his foolhardy attempt to find his mother in the dead of winter.

Gil had never experienced such a hard winter. Every trip to the outhouse was torture as the wind cut into any exposed skin with real pain, not just a sensation of coldness. For weeks the ground remained frozen as hard as stone, and between storms the snow around each settlement turned black with soot.

However, after dinner on the third Sunday of

March, Peter Cartwright put down his napkin and said to Gil, "If we don't get any more big storms in the next couple weeks, you want to take a trip up north?"

Gil's heart leaped. "Sure! But . . . I don't have enough money to get a new horse."

Cartwright stroked his chin thoughtfully. "An old woman in Springfield lost her husband last year. She had no way to take care of her horses and gave them to me, knowin' I do a lot of travelin'. There are two of 'em, none too young, but one seems pretty fit. Tell you what I'll do. I'll trade her to you in exchange for you helping me put in the crops this spring."

A relieved grin spread across Gil's face. Maybe this was his answer to prayer, after all.

Peter Cartwright didn't believe in traveling on Sunday when it could be avoided, so two weeks and a day later, they set out for the north.

As they traveled up the Illinois River, Gil tried to pick out the places he remembered from his perilous December journey. But everything looked different, and he couldn't find the cave that had kept him alive.

"Well, you were pretty wrought up, and the snow is nearly gone," Cartwright said. "Things are bound to look unfamiliar."

They arrived at Fort Clark just as it began raining. Water came down heavy for two days, melting the last of the snow and flooding all the low areas.

When it finally stopped, Cartwright said, "I had wanted to go on with you, but with this delay I need to head back. If you go on, I suggest you wait a few days until the water goes down. However, don't give up, son. As I always say, 'Never retreat till you know you can advance no farther!' "

With that they said their goodbyes, and Gil was on his own again. He waited one more day, then asked directions to Fort Armstrong, the trading post and fort near Saukenuk at the mouth of the Rock River. Most of the men told Gil to wait a little longer, but finally he convinced a corporal to ride out with him a ways.

"There's a trail, sure enough," said the blond-haired soldier with a curly mustache. "But it wouldn't be very visible this time of year, what with so much rain and all. You gotta have some landmarks to go by."

About two miles out, the corporal pointed to a stand of timber on the horizon. "Head for those trees and pray you get there before dark. A settler and his family have a cabin there, and they'll most likely be glad for your company. They can point you the right way from there. But I don't mind tellin' you that I think you're a fool to head out when the ground is so wet and soft. I wouldn't be surprised if I never see you again."

The warning sent a chill through Gil, but he took heart from Cartwright's words: "Never retreat till you can advance no farther . . ."

In a short time he was feeling more confident. His distant landmark provided all the direction he needed to progress in the right direction while making detours around the many lowlands which had turned into small lakes. He lost sight of it sometimes when he was in a ravine or valley, but when he gained high ground again, there it would be, each time a little closer.

He arrived at the grove by the middle of the afternoon and soon found the small cabin, but no one was home. Since there was still plenty of daylight, Gil thought he should travel a little farther before stopping and went to the far side of the grove to see if the path was obvious. There was no visible trail, but several miles to the northwest there was another grove of trees, and he decided that if there were any settlers in the vicinity, they would have certainly located there, so he set out.

But only a little way out onto the prairie, Gil came to a large creek that had overflowed its banks. The water spread out some two hundred yards wide. He spent over an hour wandering upstream and downstream with no success in finding a spot narrow enough to cross. At one point he rode out about a third of the way across until his horse was nearly swimming. Discouraged, he decided that it was too risky and gave up.

Back at the cabin, he found some cornmeal, which he made into pancakes, and some dried venison. It was a welcome meal after a hard day's ride, and the bed provided a comfortable sleep.

The next morning he left a coin on the table and went to check the creek again. The water level had dropped far enough that he was able to make it across by taking off his clothes and carrying them above his head, then going back to lead his horse across. Still the water came up to his neck and was terribly cold.

In the next grove he found some settlers at home, and with them was the family in whose cabin he had stayed the night before. They were holing up with their neighbors until the water subsided, and were amazed that Gil had made it across the flooded creek safely.

"I'm mighty grateful for the use of your cabin," he said. "Now, could you tell me how to get to Saukenuk?"

Gil was told that Saukenuk was on the north side of the Rock River at the point where it emptied into the Mississippi. Seeing how high the streams were, he worried that the river might be too swollen to cross.

But when he arrived at the Rock River, his concerns were relieved. Upstream was a large island in the middle of the river, and as he watched, he saw three Indian boys drive a small herd of horses into the river from the far bank. They made it easily to the island without the water even reaching the horses' bellies. In coming from the island to the bank on which he stood they encountered deeper water, but all made it safely, so Gil rode upstream to use the same ford.

The trail from the riverbank to the village took Gil through large fields that were already being prepared by some Sauk women for planting. Gil could still see some of the remains of last year's harvest: dried pumpkin vines, old cornstalks, and bean plants.

Saukenuk was much larger and more developed than Gil had ever imagined. It included nearly a hundred houses laid out neatly along two broad streets, the main one running north and south and the other running east. The two streets formed a right angle at the southern end.

Dogs barked furiously at Gil, and a few small children trailed along behind him as he rode up the main street. Women were working on their houses and paid no attention to Gil. The lodges were not the cone-shaped tepees or domed wickiups Gil had seen in small, temporary Indian villages. These summer houses were rectangular—twenty-five feet wide and sixty feet long. They were constructed from poles in the ground, and they had pitched roofs overlaid with large sheets of woven elm bark that were tied securely together. It was some of this bark that the women were replacing. The houses might not be as substantial as a log cabin, Gil thought, but they looked roomy and permanent.

Thousands of people must live here, thought Gil, but he saw few men. Finally, he came upon a half-dozen old men sitting in front of one of the lodges, smoking pipes. They were wrapped in blankets and wore bear claw necklaces. They didn't even look up when Gil reined in his horse and asked where he could find Black Hawk.

Frustrated, Gil spoke louder as though the language barrier could be bridged by volume. "Black

Hawk. Where is Black Hawk?"

That time two of them shook their heads and pointed up the street.

Gil kicked his horse into a trot until he came to a lone old man wrapping rawhide around the head of a spear. Again Gil stopped and asked him about Black Hawk, and after several moments the old Sauk replied, "*Ma-ka-tai-me-she-kia-kiak* hunting."

"Who is this Ma-ka-tak . . . or whatever you called him? Is that Black Hawk?"

The old man nodded his head, which was wrapped in a colorful cloth headdress.

"Will they be home tonight?"

"No. But soon. This is *a-paw-in-eck-kee keeshis*."

"It's what?"

"This is . . ." The old man waved his hand in front of his face searching for words. "This is . . . this is the fish-moon month. All hunters come back soon."

"Is there a white woman in the village?" Gil pressed. "I'm looking for a white woman."

The old man shook his head.

"Are you sure? Have you ever seen a white woman living among your people?"

The old man considered Gil's question and after a while said, "Yes. I have seen a white woman living with the Mesquakie."

"Where are the Mesquakie?"

The man picked up a stick and drew a line in the dirt. "River," he said, pointing toward the Rock River from which Gil had come. Then he drew another line just touching the end of the first. "Big river."

"The Mississippi?" asked Gil.

The man nodded and then poked his stick beside the "Mississippi" line not far above where the "Rock River" line joined it. "Mesquakie village."

Gil looked around, uncertain of his directions. The old Sauk pointed north, up the village's main street, and said, "That way. Be there before dark."

Gil lost no time traveling the short distance to the northern side of the peninsula dividing the Rock and the Mississippi rivers. The Mesquakie village was tiny compared to Saukenuk, and he had visited each lodge before dark. The only "white" woman he found was an old medicine woman with exceptionally white hair who smeared white clay on her face.

When Gil asked if there was a white woman living in the village, she nodded vigorously and gave him a big, toothless grin as she pounded her finger into her chest saying, "White woman, white woman!"

Gil was discouraged and ready to give up when suddenly he heard the enormous boom of a cannon followed by the faint sound of a trumpet playing taps.

"What's that?" he asked in alarm.

In her same jerky way, the woman stabbed a crooked finger toward the river and said, "Fort, fort."

Gil pushed his horse through the tall willow bushes that separated the village from the river until he was standing on the sandy shore of the Mississippi. There, in the evening's twilight, he could see an island with buildings on it and lights.

Of course! It was Fort Armstrong. He had been given directions to it as he left Fort Clark. It had never occurred to him that Fort Armstrong and Saukenuk would be only a few miles from each other.

The Mississippi was much more formidable than the Rock River. This time he tethered his horse and borrowed one of the many canoes left along the riverbank to paddle across the river. Once on the island, it didn't take him long to find the Indian agent for the area, a man named John Forsyth, who warmly welcomed him and invited him to stay for supper.

When Gil had told his story, Forsyth said, "I'm sorry I can't help you. I've been stationed here eight years and have often been in Saukenuk and most of the other Sauk and Fox villages in these parts, but—"

" 'Fox villages'?" Gil interrupted. He hadn't heard of any Fox Indians.

"Yeah, like that sorry little camp across the river."

"I thought they were called Mesquakie."

"Fox, Mesquakie, what's the difference? Mesquakie's the Indian name, I guess."

Gil felt uncomfortable. Why didn't the Indian agent call the tribe by the name the people preferred?

"Anyway," Forsyth went on, "I'm not aware of a white woman living in any of the Indian villages around these parts. If there were, she would have made herself known to me and come out by now."

"Do you think Black Hawk could have taken my

mother?"

"Possibly. Taking captives is common in war, but the Sauks are a civilized people—in spite of all this trouble we're having between them and the settlers—and I don't think they would hold a woman against her will, at least not for long."

"Maybe they sold her to some other tribe. Have you heard of any white woman, any squaw with blue eyes? My mother had blue eyes."

"Blue eyes?" Forsyth looked thoughtfully down at his plate and turned his food with his fork. "There is one blue-eyed squaw in Saukenuk. I've seen her, but I sure don't think she's a white woman."

Gil sat up in his chair and leaned forward.

Forsyth held up his hand. "Now don't go gettin' your hopes up. The Spanish came through these parts hundreds of years ago, and since then there have been the French and the British, let alone American traders. It takes only one white man to pass his blue eyes along to later generations. Blue eyes can crop up almost anywhere. They don't necessarily mean anything."

"I know, but . . . it might be her."

"Listen, son, I've seen her. She's just a regular squaw."

But when Gil went to sleep that night in Forsyth's cabin, he couldn't help dreaming about his mother, the Blue-eyed Moon Singer. For the first time in years an image of her face seemed to float before him: blue eyes . . . soft, white skin . . . dark, wavy hair. And she smiled at him.

Chapter 12

The Blue-eyed Moon Singer

IN THE MORNING, Gil did not wait to eat breakfast. As soon as the sun blinked over the horizon, he was at the waterfront, pushing off in the canoe for the southern bank.

After beaching the flimsy craft, he retrieved his horse and rode through the quiet Mesquakie village where thin tendrils of smoke rose from some of the fire pits. Even the dogs were too sleepy to make a fuss over him.

He rode on through the woods, across the Sauk horse pasture, and over the empty vegetable fields until he arrived at the outskirts of Saukenuk, his heart racing.

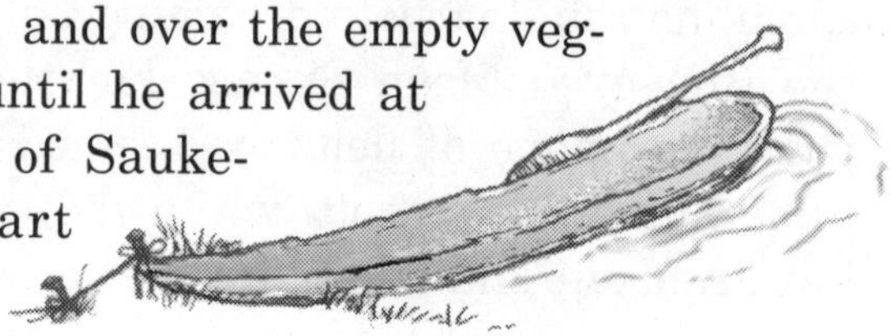

Mama . . . Mama . . . you've just gotta be here, he thought. *I missed you yesterday, but I'll find you today.*

He dismounted and tried to calm himself as he walked down the street, looking carefully at each house. People were starting to stir. A two-year-old pushed aside the door flap and toddled out, rubbing his eyes with the back of his hands. A few feet away from the house, he stood watching two puppies play tug-of-war with what looked like a chewed-up moccasin. The toddler reached down and pulled the tail of one puppy until it whined pitifully. An older sister rushed out scolding him.

Farther down the street, Gil saw a woman carrying two kettles hanging from a pole across her shoulder. She was headed toward the river.

When he got to the lodge of the man who had spoken English with him the day before, he approached the door listening for wake-up sounds. But all he heard was slow, deep snoring. He looked around and cleared his throat. The snoring did not change.

Gil walked on past a few more houses, then returned to the old man's lodge. Still the snoring continued. He coughed and shuffled his feet to make a little noise. No luck.

Finally, he sat down, convinced that he would have to wait for the man to wake up on his own. The snoring continued. He waited. And waited.

Then suddenly the snoring stopped, the door flap swung back, and the old man spoke—all at once.

"Why you not go away?"

"What? You knew I was out here?"

"Of course. I see through crack. You come, go, come back, sit down. Why you bother me?"

"I'm trying to find my mother!" Gil said through clenched teeth. He shook his hands in front of him, fingers spread, as though he were about to grab the old man by the throat.

The door flap closed, and from within the old man said, "Go away. You have bad spirit."

"Oh, no!" moaned Gil as he spun around and clinched his fists in frustration. "Listen, I'm sorry. I'm sorry." He returned to the door and was going to knock but didn't know whether that was the Sauk custom. Instead, he leaned his head close to the door and said, "Hello? I need your help. Can you please open the door?"

Gil waited.

Finally, the man pulled door flap again. "You still here?"

"Yeah. I thought you said you could see through the crack."

"I can. But *why* you still here?"

"Look. I need your help. I'm trying to find my mother. Do you know a squaw in the village with blue eyes?"

The old man stared at Gil without one flicker of change in his expression. He continued to stare while Gil tried to figure out whether he had misunderstood, whether he was thinking, or whether he was just being stubborn.

"Well?" said Gil when his patience ran out.

"She lives in that lodge." He pointed back up the street to the house where the little boy had come out and pulled the puppy's tail.

"She does?" asked Gil in amazement as the two puppies came racing around the front of the house.

"Why do you ask me if you are not going to believe my answer?" And the old Sauk yanked the door flap closed again.

Gil approached the house of the blue-eyed woman cautiously. Was his mother within? Or was she—as John Forsyth had suggested—simply a Sauk woman who happened to have some blue-eyed, white explorer for an ancestor?

The little boy was outside again, teasing the puppies with a stick. He was naked except for a dirty buckskin top. When he noticed Gil approaching the house, he stopped his play and stared at him. Then he asked some question—unintelligible to Gil—and pointed back over his shoulder toward the lodge.

"Yes, yes. Your house?" said Gil, trying to communicate. "Is that your house?"

The boy babbled off a long sentence in the Sauk language, or at least what Gil guessed was Sauk.

"Is . . . your . . . mommy . . . home?" Gil said each word slowly and distinctly as though that would help the two-year-old understand English. He watched the child expectantly and then realized how foolish that was.

Finally, he sat on the ground and leaned against a pole of the fish-drying rack. The boy continued playing with the puppies. Soon the older sister Gil had seen earlier came out carrying a tightly woven basket and headed down the street. She looked at Gil and frowned as she passed. Gil guessed that she was probably eight or nine.

In a moment, two boys came out—maybe four and six—followed by a woman. She spoke rapidly to them, pointing to a small pile of wood on the ground near the fire pit, and then pointed toward the hill behind the village. It was obvious to Gil that she was unhappy they had allowed the supply to get so low and wanted them to gather more.

They ran off, and the woman turned to look briefly at Gil.

It was the first time he had seen her face.

It was true. She had blue eyes!

Gil stared hard, and the intensity of his gaze held the woman's attention for a moment, and then she turned away and went back into the house.

Gil's heart sank. She looked as Indian as any squaw in the village. The beads and strips of cloth braided into her hair looked like those of all the other women. Her skin was dark and leathery, lined with strain and toil. She looked old—not at all like the beautiful, smooth-faced mother Gil had seen in his dream the night before.

She was just a Sauk squaw.

Or was she? *Maybe her skin is just a little lighter than the other Sauks,* Gil imagined. *Maybe it's just the rough living that's made it leathery and old looking. She'd be older now, so maybe it's logical for her hair to have some gray in it. And maybe my dream image wasn't even an accurate memory.*

The woman came out again and began to stir the ashes in the fire pit. Then she added twigs and soon had a blaze.

"Do you speak English?" Gil ventured. He had to be sure it wasn't her.

She did not respond.

"I was talking to the old man across the way, and he said you have blue eyes."

She turned and looked blankly at him as the two-year-old carried one of the puppies over and dropped it in Gil's lap.

Did she understand me and turn to show me her eyes? Or was she just looking around to see if her child was safe with a stranger? There had not been the slightest flicker of response in her expression; she had simply looked in his direction.

After a while, Gil tried again. "Is Black Hawk . . . did he . . . do you . . . ?" But he didn't know what to say. Was he her captor? Was he her husband? To whom did these children belong? It was all so overwhelming that Gil didn't know what to say. And the woman made no response.

In a few moments the squaw went back into the house.

The toddler carried the other puppy over to Gil and held its nose up to the one in Gil's lap. He seemed as if he was trying to get them to kiss or fight. After a few seconds, the one in the boy's arms began squirming and soon broke free and ran off.

The child chased it, but the dog ran faster around in a circle, then around the corner of the building and back, and then around the fire pit.

The toddler tripped and fell, his hand touching a hot rock in the fire ring. He wailed.

Gil leaped up and pulled the child back from the fire. The door flap opened, and the woman looked out. Gil held the child out toward her, but by then his crying had changed to indicate he was not in any real pain. She just looked at Gil and let the flap close again.

Gil sat down with the boy on his lap and rocked back and forth. The child kept fussing until Gil, not knowing what else to do, started to sing.

I see the moon, and the moon sees me.
God bless the moon, and God bless me. . . .

Suddenly, from inside the lodge, Gil heard a soft voice continuing the song . . .

There's grace in the cabin
And grace in the hall,
And the grace of God is over us all.

Slowly the flap of the lodge swung open a crack, and the woman peeked out. Tears were running down her face. In perfect English she pleaded, "How do you know that song? That's my song!"

Startled, Gil said, "I don't know . . . I've always known it. My mother used to sing it to me."

“Your mother? But I made up the tune—and most of the words, too. It’s mine.”

Gil’s mouth went dry. “Mama?” he asked, setting

the child down and scrambling to his feet.

The flap closed.

"Mama! It's me, Gil . . . Gilbert Hamilton. Don't you remember? I've come to get you. Come out!"

But Gil's only answer was deep sobbing from within the lodge.

It took Gil the rest of the morning to get his mother to come out of her lodge. The older boys came back with a pile of firewood and then ran off to play. The sister brought a basket of dried pumpkin and made a porridge.

Finally, the flap opened and Gil's mother came out. Her face was streaked with tears. "It's such a shock," she whispered. "I thought you were dead! Killed in the battle."

Slowly, Gil and his mother began to put the story together. The horror of the war, her husband's death, her own capture, and her assumption that Gil was dead, too, had left Audry Hamilton so traumatized that at first she could not even attempt an escape. She was like a zombie, walking through a bad dream wherever the Sauks led her.

By the time she calmed down and began to recover her wits, the tribe had traveled hundreds of miles west to their wilderness home, and she had no idea where she was. At that point escape seemed impossible.

Two years passed. It had not been Black Hawk

but another brave who claimed her after he lost his own squaw when she was in childbirth. He proved to be a kind and honorable man and had asked Audry's permission to become her husband. In time, she had agreed, and they were married.

By the time Audry came in contact with white trappers and other English-speaking people, there seemed to be no reason to go home. She thought her family had been killed and her home destroyed in the fighting. She knew her former husband's relatives in Kentucky didn't like her, and she was pregnant with a new baby, so she made up her mind to remain with the Sauk people.

Gil cried when he heard the story. After all these years, he finally understood why his mother never came to him, never wrote to him, never sent for him.

They both cried.

"Look at us . . . blubbering away like two springs on a hillside," said Gil. "This is the happiest day of my life. I've found you! Finally, you can come home with me. Now you have a white family again."

"Oh, Gil," she moaned, as a look of great sorrow washed over her face. "What about my babies?" She looked around blankly. "I cannot go off and leave them . . . or my husband."

"But they're Indian! They'll be fine here."

"What does that matter? They are mine. I cannot leave them."

"But . . . I'm yours, too. What about me?"

"Oh, Gil." His mother bit her lower lip and looked off toward the river. "Gil . . . you're grown, almost a man, and a fine one at that. You can take care of yourself. They cannot."

Gil stayed in the Sauk village for a whole week, but no matter how he pled and argued, his mother would not go with him. He considered staying with her permanently, but he knew that was ridiculous. He couldn't become a Sauk. Besides, John Forsyth had warned him about increasing tension between the Sauks and the American Government. His mother explained that the government wanted to move the Indians west of the Mississippi according to an old treaty.

"Black Hawk claims it was a faulty treaty," she said. "He says the Americans tricked our old chiefs into signing it by getting them drunk. Our people don't want to leave Saukenuk. If there's gonna be trouble, I can't be away from my children."

At week's end, Audry Hamilton—blue-eyed squaw—walked her oldest son to the bank of the Rock River.

"I'll be back to visit you . . . often," he said hoarsely.

Quietly she lifted her hand as he climbed onto his horse and guided it out into the river's shallows.

Chapter 13

The Potawatomi Mission

BACK IN SANGAMON COUNTY, as Gil helped Peter Cartwright plant his spring crops, he was a tumbler of emotions. He had found his mother. She was safe, and he had answered the main mysteries of his life. All that brought satisfaction, but somehow the deep longing for home still tugged like weighted fishhooks on his heart.

He mentioned it to Cartwright one afternoon when they had finished plowing the barley field. The two were sitting beneath an apple tree they had found on the farm—maybe one Johnny Appleseed had planted.

"You think you'd be happier if she came down here and

made a home for you?" Cartwright asked.

"Sure, wouldn't anyone? I mean, I never had a home that was really my own."

"What if you had? What would you be doing now?"

"I don't know."

"Well, what are most boys your age doing? Are they looking forward to continuing to live with their mothers for years and years?"

"Well, no. I guess they're thinking about headin' out, seeing the world, makin' a life of their own."

"So what would you do if you talked her into comin' down here to live in Springfield or St. Louis?"

Gil shrugged.

After a few moments he said, "I just want a little of what everyone else has. Then I'd be satisfied."

Cartwright didn't answer in words. Instead, he began to hum, and then he broke into song.

How happy every child of grace,
Who knows his sins forgiven!
"This earth," he cries, "is not my place,
I seek my place in heaven."

Gil remembered the song from one of the early camp meetings he had attended in Kentucky. Its haunting tune tugged on those fishhooks still stuck in his heart, and a lump came to his throat.

Cartwright sang the song three times, and then he said, "You see, Gil, even for those who grow up in a good home, it's not their permanent place. Whether our home is good or bad or even if we don't have one at all, God's whole purpose is to plant within us a hunger. When we're older we hanker for our childhood home, or we wish it could have been kinder, or—as in your case—we long for what we never had. It's all the same. It's a longing God plants within us, His way of drawin' us to himself and peace with Him."

"Yeah, but . . ." Gil didn't know what he wanted to say, but the rough old preacher waited patiently. Finally, Gil continued, "I guess you're right in sayin' I can never have the home I long for with my mother. I can see that's out of the question now."

"That's the first step, Gil. But if you get caught there, you'll just feel sorry for yourself and angry at God, thinkin' you got the raw end of life. That makes a person bitter."

Cartwright let Gil chew on that for a while, then he continued. "The good news is, God has something better for us—a relationship that's not dependent on creating paradise some place here on earth."

It was a big bite for Gil. It meant accepting that life with his mother was not what he really longed for. He tossed the idea around in his mind. As much as he wished he could've had a normal home life, he knew Peter was right. He longed for something more. But it was hard to give up the old dream, even though he knew it wouldn't satisfy him.

Finally, he said, "I guess I'm ready, Reverend Cartwright. I want heaven to be my home and God to be my Father."

✧ ✧ ✧ ✧

Each spring Gil traveled to Saukenuk to visit his mother. Peter Cartwright often made the trip with him, preaching to the Indians whenever he could.

One day, when Gil and Cartwright arrived at Saukenuk, Gil's mother was not to be found. The village was nearly empty because most of the men and some of the women were still out on the winter hunt, but they knew that Audry seldom went out on those trips, which could last a month or two. Finally, one of the villagers told them that she was up on the bluff at the burial grounds. Her husband had died. They sent word to her, but she would not interrupt her period of mourning.

Gil thought this might be the occasion for getting his mother to return to white society, but when he came back a few months later to talk with her, she said no. "It's important for me to raise my children in their native tradition," she said firmly. "I will not try to make white people of them."

Gil nodded. He knew she was right . . . and realized for the first time that he was interested in what was best for her. He no longer felt the need to get her to create a home for him. He felt at home with God.

But troubles with the government were worsening. White settlers were moving into the northern part of Illinois more and more rapidly, and they didn't like sharing the land with the Indians. Almost weekly there were incidents: whites claiming Indians came onto their farms uninvited; Indians claiming that whites killed or stole their horses.

“It’s gonna bust wide open pretty soon,” Gil told Cartwright when he returned to Sangamon County. “Mama says Black Hawk is refusing to move, and I don’t blame him. It’s a dirty rotten thing the government is trying to do to the Sauks, pushing them onto a tiny reservation out west. A lot of the Sauks are rallying around Black Hawk and talking war, but . . . I hate to think of my mother there in the middle of trouble.”

“I’ve been thinkin’,” Cartwright said, “several of these Illinois Indians—the Sauks, the Mesquakie, the Potawatomi—have shown interest in the gospel. But it’s hard to create a circuit to minister to them because they are always away from their village, off on some hunting or fishing expedition. They’re never home. But they sure do love camp meetings.”

Gil gave him a curious look, wondering why the preacher had changed the subject to talk about the problems of a preaching circuit among the Indians. “What do you mean, ‘they love camp meetings’?”

“Well, they do; they’re always getting together to have a rendezvous with some other tribe. It’s a way of life with them. They were doing it long before we ever thought of it. Now, what if we set up a permanent ‘camp meeting’ to which they could come whenever they wanted?” Cartwright grinned. “For the sake of the denomination, we could call it a mission.”

At the mention of the word “permanent,” Gil said, “Would it be possible for some Indians to live there?”

“Of course.”

Suddenly Gil got the drift of Cartwright’s plan.

"Then," he said eagerly, "if war came, there'd be a place of refuge where those who didn't want to be in the middle of the fighting could find safety . . . people like my mother and her children."

"Right, and I got just the man to head it up, too," said Cartwright. "Jesse Walker, an old circuit rider who wants to settle down. He would make a good missionary, and I think the Illinois Conference of the Methodist Episcopal Church would sponsor it."

In the months that followed, Peter Cartwright worked hard to start the mission, but his efforts were hindered by the fact that he was also entering politics, trying to get elected to the Illinois General Assembly. He had a strong opponent, a tall lanky fellow named Abraham Lincoln who had just moved to Illinois from Kentucky. Cartwright, who was the better known of the two, won the election, but in the process Cartwright and Lincoln became friends.

"But what about the mission?" Gil asked Cartwright one day. "It seems like you're so busy with all this political stuff that your church work is suffering." Gil was more worried than ever about his mother. He'd just heard that white settlers had shot an unarmed Sauk. War was inevitable.

"Maybe you're right," said Cartwright, frowning. "After this term, I don't know whether I'll do it again. Abe Lincoln is a fine young man. We agree on almost everything, and he's a lawyer . . . maybe he's more suited to politics.

"As for the mission," he continued, "I've got good news. We found a place on the Fox River for the

Potawatomi Mission—that's what it's gonna be called—and Walker's ready to go. But he'll need some help. Whaddya think, Gil—would you like to work there?"

"Sure!" Gil said eagerly, and then blinked in amazement. Just that morning he'd read a verse in the Book of Matthew: "Seek ye first the kingdom of God, and his righteousness; and all these things shall be added unto you." Cartwright had helped him seek his true home with Jesus, and God had given him the peace he'd desired for so long. Now, he was going to be with his mother—not so she could give *him* a home, but so he could give *her* one.

More About Peter Cartwright

THE AMERICAN HISTORIAN, Edward Eggleston, says, "More than anyone else, the early circuit preachers brought order out of chaos. In no other class was the real heroic character so finely displayed."

One of the most colorful and successful was Peter Cartwright. Shortly after his birth in Virginia on September 1, 1785, his family moved to Kentucky. On the way, seven families who lagged behind the caravan were massacred by Indians.

The Cartwrights finally settled in Logan County, only a mile from the Tennessee border, in an area known as "Rogues' Harbor" because of the large number of outlaws who lived there.

Peter grew up gambling, fighting, and racing horses, but when he was only fifteen years old, he attended a new event in the area: a camp-meeting revival. There he became convicted of his sin and gave his life to Christ.

Peter's conversion was dramatic, and he testified about it whenever possible. Others noticed. In the fall of 1802, as he was turning seventeen, Peter's family moved three counties farther west. When he asked the leaders of his Methodist Episcopal Church for a letter to transfer his church membership, he received instead a letter commissioning him to create a new circuit in that unchurched wilderness.

Built strong enough (in his words) "to wear out a dozen thrashing machines," Cartwright rode circuits that took him away from home from four to six weeks at a time bringing the gospel to rural families in Kentucky, Tennessee, Indiana, Ohio, and Illinois.

Periodically, there were camp meetings that gathered people in each region for an extended time of preaching, teaching, and fellowship.

Peter married Frances Gaines on August 18, 1808. Five years later they moved to a farm near Hopkinsville, not far from his childhood home in Logan County, Kentucky. They subsequently had nine children, though they tragically lost nine-year-old Cynthia when a tree fell on her following the wagon accident while they were moving to Illinois in 1824 to escape the evil influences of slavery.

While Peter Cartwright can be admired for boldly preaching the gospel and opposing slavery, gambling, and drunkenness, he (and most preachers of that day) engaged in many petty disputes. Baptists clashed with Presbyterians. Presbyterians argued with Methodists. And Peter Cartwright fought them all. His methods, while often humorous, succeeded most often in insulting his opponents. At a stocky two hundred pounds, if real troublemakers, mockers, or religious cultists tried to disrupt his camp meetings, he was not above disposing of them physically if he could not outwit them.

Cartwright was not highly educated or impressed with the value of formal seminary training for ministers. "What we need," he said, "are preachers who can mount a stump, a block, or an old log, or stand in the bed of a wagon, and without a note or manuscript, quote, expound, and apply the Word of God to the hearts and consciences of the people." And he was just such a man, riding the trail for fifty-three years over tens of thousands of miles!

He died at his farm in Pleasant Plains, Illinois, on September 25, 1872, just after his eighty-seventh birthday.

Some modern readers may be surprised at the idea of lions living in Illinois as suggested by Gil Hamilton's trip up the Illinois River. However, in 1820, at Rock Island, Illinois, George Davenport of the American Fur Company, bought two hundred cougar pelts from the local Indians.

While the first few words of the song "I See the Moon" come from a traditional Appalachian verse, the last part of the song (and the accompanying tune) are used courtesy of Lois Shuford, who sang it years ago as a lullaby to our daughter Rachel.